Kindling Flames
GATHERING TINDER

JULIE WETZEL

Crimson Tree Publishing

Kindling Flames
Copyright ©2014 Julie Wetzel
All rights reserved.

ISBN: 978-1-63422-013-2
Cover Design by: Marya Heiman
Typography by: Courtney Nuckels
Editing by: Cynthia Shepp

I'd like to dedicate this book to my sister, Amanda, and the sailors from the maiden deployment of the USS George H.W. Bush (CVN 77). Without you this story would never have happened.
May you find calm waves to bring you safely home once more.

Prologue

RUPERT SURVEYED THE CARNAGE, WHILE THE SCREAMS OF approaching sirens split the air. Flames licked at the night sky as they consumed the once beautiful home. Stepping back into the shadows of the neighboring houses, he watched as the fire truck roared up and spilled out first responders to quench the raging inferno. The light of the fire glistened off the bloody mess on the lawn that had once been his friend.

Turning from the chaos, Rupert slipped into the night, trying to wrap his mind around events. It had been nearly a month since the first of his people went missing. It took two days to determine that the bloody chunks strewn across the lawn of the first unexplained fire had been the missing man. The body had only been identified by the cell phone and wallet found in the mix. The police concluded that he came over to help his neighbor and was caught up in whatever had flash-burnt the home. Rupert had called for patrols of the surrounding area in an attempt to find what was responsible for the death. Now, a second fire had broken out, and another of his was dead. But how? He hadn't been away from Brian for very long. What could reduce a body to fist-sized bits in a matter of minutes?

A tawny wolf appeared out of the darkness to rub against his leg. Rupert scrubbed his fingers into the scruff at the back of the wolf's neck. "They will pay," he promised. Whoever had done this would pay dearly. Rupert's mind turned on the possibilities. There was no way a human could have killed like that, but what could? A rampant werewolf? A crazed wolf could have caused that degree of destruction, but it would have taken much longer than the few minutes allotted. A vampire? They had the strength and speed, but how had they gotten the fire to engulf the home so quickly? The fay? There were certainly possibilities there.

Rupert turned back to where he had left his van. He could do no more until the police finished processing the scene. Later, he would bring others back to see if they could find anything the police had missed. It had to stop. Something capable of this couldn't be left loose in the city. If they couldn't figure out what it was, he could only think of one person that would have the resources to help.

Rupert's eyes turned north towards the heart of Brenton. Darien could help if he could just be persuaded into action.

1

DARIEN LOOKED UP FROM HIS DESK TO THE YOUNG WOMAN waiting and sighed. This was the fourth personal assistant the temp agency had sent this month, and she didn't seem any more promising than the last three. His own personnel office had already offered six possible candidates, all of whom had been unable to handle the task of dealing with his hectic life. Oh, how he longed for Marianna to come back, even if she was five months pregnant with triplets. If only she hadn't fallen in love with that rascal, she would be here, running his life, not stuck in bed with a high-risk pregnancy and three brats to look forward to. Letting out another sigh, he read over the girl's credentials one more time.

He read the name from the file. "Victoria Westernly." He saw the slight purse of the woman's lips as he used her full name, but she kept a cool and confident air. "Do you go by Victoria?" he asked.

"I'll answer to Victoria, but I prefer Vicky," she answered.

Darien wrote the nickname on her file, disappointed that she would shorten such an elegant name.

Continuing on, he looked at her schooling. "Mid-State University?" he asked, reading over her course list. It was a local school, well known, and her marks were good.

"Yes, sir," Vicky answered politely.

She still stood confidently, but Darien could smell her fear. He hadn't gotten where he was without learning to detect the subtle tang of adrenaline. Raising his eyebrow at her, she straightened a little more. He considered her for a moment longer before continuing. "All right, Miss Westernly, I understand this is your first time as a personal assistant."

Vicky nodded and took a breath to relay her job history, but Darien stopped her with a wave of his hand. She let the air out and shut her mouth, waiting for her potential boss to speak again.

Darien liked that she could follow simple instructions without having them explained. Wanting to see how much the girl would fidget, he tested her patience by flipping through her entire file one more time.

He watched her carefully for a few minutes more, pretending to read. Every now and then, her eyes would be drawn to something in the room, but they would quickly come back to him. The only major movement he detected was when Vicky shifted her weight from one foot to the other as her legs tired from standing in the same place for too long. There were two very nice leather chairs in front of his desk, but he had purposely forgotten to offer her a seat to see how she would handle it. He was pleased to see she hadn't taken one without being offered. The only other thing he noted was the incessant movement of her thumb as she scratched the pad of her middle finger, waiting for him to answer.

4

Had he been a normal human, Darien might never have detected the slight, nervous fidget from where Vicky hid it in her folded hands.

"One last question." Darien looked up and locked eyes with the woman. "What's sitting on the corner of the desk just outside this room?"

Vicky cocked her head and gave the man an odd look as she searched her mind for the answer. She had spent thirty minutes sitting in that room, studying the desk. "A glass vase filled with water. There was blue gravel in the bottom and some kind of water plant growing from the top. It had a red beta in it," Vicky answered, picturing the desk.

Darien made a noise in his throat and marked something on her file.

"Oh, and there was a vase next to it."

His eyes lifted at this unexpected answer. "A vase?" he asked.

"Yes, it was about six inches tall with a square, fluted opening at the top." Vicky described the trinket as best she could remember. "Brown. Very pretty. It had some kind of beaded thing around the neck."

Darien lifted an eyebrow at how well the girl remembered the details of the items on the desk. He wasn't surprised Marianna had left the knickknack when she had packed her things away. She hadn't liked the present very much when he gave it to her. Darien read the words he had written and drew a line through them. 'Only sees the obvious' definitely did not describe someone who noticed the little vase next to that elaborate fish bowl.

"Very well, Miss Westernly." He closed the file and slipped it into his desk drawer. Pulling a black messenger bag from under his desk, he stood up. "We'll see how it works out." Darien noticed the sigh of relief that issued from her, but she still managed to keep the emotion from her face. He stepped around the desk and held the leather bag out to her.

Vicky took it gingerly from his hand.

"This contains my entire life. It'll be your job to keep up with everything." Reaching into his pocket, Darien pulled out a phone for his new personal assistant. "Here. Keep this with you. If it rings, day or night, answer it. You're on salary now, so you work when I tell you to."

The young woman nodded, taking the phone from her new boss.

"The desk and computer in the other room are yours. The password's in the bag. Feel free to change it to whatever you like."

Vicky's eyes widened a little as she took in what he said.

"You're here to keep my life in order," he continued. "Get your work done, and any free time is yours to do with as you please. However, I don't want you to think this means your job will be easy. I'm a very busy man."

He paused for a moment to let Vicky process this information. "Be here at seven. We stay till we're done. There will be some weekends, but I'll let you know in advance so you can make arrangements. If there are any problems, bring them straight to me. Otherwise, do what I say when I say it. Oh, and if you don't already have a passport, get one. Is that clear?"

"Yes, sir," Vicky started.

"Ritter," Darien corrected her.

"Yes, Mr. Ritter," she quickly restated. "I'll do my best."

Darien took a moment to actually look at the

well-dressed woman standing in front of him. He had glanced her over as soon as she came in, but now, he really studied her. She had a shapely face and lightly done makeup. Her eyes were the grayish-blue of a rainy sky, and her dark blonde hair was twisted up and held by a pin to the back of her head. He guessed it would fall well past her shoulders if he yanked the pin from it. Long and lean for her height of around 5'4", she wasn't what he would call beautiful, but she was well built and could turn heads in the right outfit. Overall, a pleasant girl to look at. Darien nodded his approval.

She stood in front of him and waited until he was done.

"If you have any questions, please let me know." Darien dismissed her and returned to his chair.

Vicky clutched her new possessions as she waited for him to notice her again.

He turned questioning eyes up to the woman he had expected to leave. "Was there something else?" he asked, slightly annoyed she hadn't left to settle in.

Vicky nodded. "Where's the charger?"

Darien gave her a strange look, not comprehending the question.

Vicky held up the phone. "The charger."

Enlightenment crossed his face as he realized his omission. He reached down to the power strip under his desk to pull the cord out and wadded it up. "Here." Darien handed the wire to her.

Vicky took it with a very polite 'thank you' and turned to go to her new desk.

He watched the door close behind the woman he'd just entrusted his human life with. Maybe she wasn't going to be worthless after all.

7

Vicky closed the door behind her and took a deep breath to clear out the terror haunting her. When the temp agency sent her for the assistant's position at Ritter Enterprises, she hadn't expected it to be with the main man himself. Anyone in the business world could tell you that Darien Ritter was the CEO and owner of a worldwide shipping company. He had inherited the firm when his father, Michael Ritter, had died suddenly in a plane crash. Darien was the epitome of wealth and power, a philanthropist known for backing small businesses that piqued his interest, and was high on the list of Forbes' most eligible bachelors. He stood six feet tall at around 180 pounds of solid muscle, with rich, brown hair, and the most beautiful green eyes Vicky had ever seen. What the magazines failed to mention was his voice. It was like black velvet—commanding, almost tangible, yet it warmed her to her toes. Vicky drew another deep, calming breath and took the leather bag to her new desk.

Noting the comfort of the expensive leather chair, Vicky turned her mind to the job she was hired for. A thorough investigation of the leather satchel left her slightly stunned. In addition to the day planner, address book, and notepad she had expected, there was also an account ledger, a checkbook, and two wallets. She knew the man was rich, but the balance in his bank ledger nearly caused her heart palpitations. And what man needed seven different credit cards? The part that really blew her mind was the thick wad of cash she'd discovered in the second wallet. Who trusted someone they'd just met with nearly four thousand dollars? She had stashed the money back in the bag as quickly as she could. The last thing she found was a large key ring. It looked to be a set of master keys to everything the man owned, but none of them were marked as to where they went. Vicky packed everything neatly back into the bag and stowed it under the desk.

It was stunning to see how much of Darien's life she had been entrusted with. As if making sure he was where he needed to be wasn't a big enough responsibility, she was also expected to take care of his personal expenses. Vicky sighed heavily, pulled the computer over, and flipped the top open. When she entered the password she had found in the notebook, she was greeted by the ugliest picture of a cat in a tutu that she had ever seen. Obviously, his last assistant had no taste at all. She switched the wallpaper to a stock picture of Stonehenge, cleared out the remnants of the last user, and changed the password to something she could easily remember. A quick search revealed several files holding the information from the credit cards and an electronic copy of the checking ledger from her bag. She looked over the files and decided there was something she could already do.

Vicky pulled out the leather-bound ledger and updated its electronic twin. Next, she pulled out the credit card receipts that had been tucked into the back of one of the wallets. Those files were also behind, so she sorted out the receipts and logged them.

Once finished, she mulled over what to do with the stack of papers. She looked through the desk drawers, but found no answers. Plucking up her courage, she did the only thing she could think of—go ask.

⬥⬥⬥

"Come in," Darien called to the tentative knock at his door. What could his new assistant want? Vicky

9

stepped into the room and approached his desk. He kind of liked that the girl was a little afraid of him. It was a nice change from the last two temps that had annoyed him by spending every moment they could with him. The last one had even propositioned him before he had sent her packing.

"Sorry for disturbing you, Mr. Ritter, but what do I do with these?" The young woman held the stack of receipts out for him to see.

"There are some files on the computer where they'll need to be logged," Darien explained.

Vicky tilted her head and looked at him. "What do I do with them after that? Is there a folder somewhere where you keep them, or do they just get tossed?"

Darien looked at his new assistant, surprised to learn she had already jumped into her job with both feet. "We keep them until the bill comes in." He pointed to a short cabinet in the corner of his office. "File them over there for now. They'll get pulled out and shredded once the bill is paid."

Vicky thanked him for the help and quickly sorted the slips into the files before turning to leave. Pausing at the door, she turned back to the man watching her.

"It's almost lunchtime. Did you need anything to eat?"

Darien was staggered at the woman's consideration. Marianna use to remind him to eat, but the last three temps hadn't. He quickly recovered from his surprise and answered, "I'm fine, thank you, but you're welcome to take an hour for lunch. There's a café on the fifth floor."

Vicky nodded her understanding and turned to go.

"Miss Westernly…"

She stopped and looked back.

"Thank you."

Vicky smiled brightly at him and slipped from the room.

Darien was shocked again by her response. He had to change his view of this young woman. Her face lit up when she smiled, making her amazingly beautiful. How had he missed that during the time she had been in his office?

At twelve thirty, Darien decided to go get some coffee. He didn't need to eat like a normal person, and the caffeine did nothing for him, but he still loved his coffees.

He slipped from his office to get a caramel macchiato from the café downstairs. The sight of his new assistant at her desk, munching half a sandwich and playing Minesweeper, stopped him in his tracks.

Vicky looked up from her meager meal and entertainment to find her new boss staring at her. She swallowed the bite of sandwich that had just gone dry in her mouth and dropped the rest so it was hidden behind her desk. "Is there something I can do for you, Mr. Ritter?" she asked, in the best professional voice she could muster with sandwich crumbs spread across her lap.

Darien considered her for a moment. "I did say you could take the lunch hour to get something at the café?" He was sure he had made himself clear.

Vicky raised the sandwich up to show him. "I didn't know what to expect, so I brought something from home," she admitted shyly.

Darien chuckled to himself. Glancing over the meal she brought, his eyes caught on the little fruits on her desk. "What's that?" Darien pointed at what looked like wrinkly, mini oranges.

Vicky looked where he was pointing and set her sandwich down. "They're clementines." Picking up one of the citrus fruits, she split open the peel to reveal the cute, little pieces inside, and held the whole thing out for him to take.

Darien pulled one of the slices out and slipped it into his mouth. His eyes lit up at the burst of juice that was close to an orange, yet not quite the same. "Oh wow," he exclaimed.

Vicky smiled at his reaction.

Darien popped a second piece into his mouth before realizing he was eating his new assistant's lunch. "I'm sorry." He tried to give the unfinished clementine back to her, but she waved it away with a smile.

"I have more, enjoy it." Vicky felt a little more relaxed at seeing the great man that terrified her act just as human as the next guy.

"Thank you." Darien accepted the gift and paused for a moment. "I'm heading down to get some coffee. Would you like to join me, Miss Westernly?"

Vicky jumped at the opportunity to learn more about the man she would be working for. She quickly packed her lunch away and stuck it in the top drawer of the desk. Pushing the laptop closed, she picked up the bag she had been charged with.

Darien smiled to himself as he watched the protective way Vicky slipped the bag over her shoulder so she could easily carry it without losing it.

Munching on the clementine, he led Vicky through the building, pointing out things she would need to know. Whenever someone spoke to him or waved, Darien told

Vicky their name and what they did in the company. By the time they reached the fifth floor café, Vicky's head was spinning with the sheer quantity of information he had thrown at her. The locations and their functions were easy, but the names and faces he paraded past her were just too much to handle in one go. Darien ended the tour by stepping up to the counter at the café.

"The usual, Mr. Ritter?" asked the barista, smiling at the handsome CEO.

"Make it two, please, Sue," he answered the spunky girl. "This is my new personal assistant, Miss Victoria Westernly." Darien presented Vicky for Sue to look over.

Vicky considered the petite woman with short, orangish-brown hair. She was sure the cute girl couldn't be more the eighteen or nineteen.

"It's nice to meet you, Miss Westernly." Sue smiled warmly at Vicky as she retrieved the things to make the coffees.

Vicky returned the smile and the greeting.

When finished, Sue placed the drinks in Darien's hands. "Here you go, Mr. Ritter."

"Thank you very much, Sue." Darien started to leave.

Vicky stood there, gaping at him. "It was a pleasure to meet you," she called to the girl behind the counter as she rushed to catch up with her new boss.

Sipping on his drink, Darien held one of the coffees out so Vicky could take it. She looked at the cup before sipping on it gingerly to find it was delicious.

"I own this building and everything in it, so I don't pay for anything at the café," Darien explained to his companion. "And since you are now my personal assistant, you don't, either." He hadn't extended this privilege to the previous temps. She hadn't even been there for a full day, and Vicky had already exceeded his expectations. "If anyone says anything to you about it, let me know. I'll take care of it. Understand?" He gave the wide-eyed woman walking next to him a pointed look.

"Yes, Mr. Ritter." It was the only response she could give the powerful man, and the only one he would have accepted.

"So what do I have scheduled for the day?" Darien asked, wanting to see how well his new assistant had done her homework.

Vicky proceeded to rattle off the list of meetings that filled the rest of the afternoon without having to pull out the planner. He smiled into his coffee. This woman looked to be exactly what he needed to take Marianna's place. And to think, this was the first time she'd ever worked as a PA.

Darien left Vicky at her desk and went back into his office to finish preparing for his meetings.

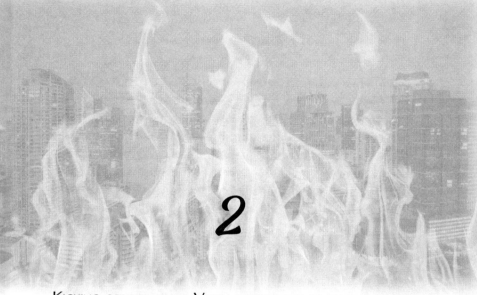

2

KICKING OFF HER HEELS, VICKY FLOPPED DOWN ON THE WORN couch just inside her small apartment. Glad that her day had finally ended, all she wanted to do was go to bed, but she had to find food first. If tomorrow were going to be as hellish as today was, she would need all the strength she could get.

Vicky pulled the messenger bag off and dropped it to the floor next to the couch. She had been reluctant to take the important man's life home, but Darien had insisted she keep it with her at all times. Turning her mind back over the hectic day, she levered herself from the cushions to scrounge in her kitchen for something edible.

She couldn't believe how insane Darien's life was. Vicky had followed him through eight meetings, across every floor of the building without hitting the elevators, and scribbled enough notes to fill ten pages of her notebook. She needed to get one of those pocket recorders so she could keep up with the man who spoke lighting fast as he walked just a hair quicker than she could move. If she weren't careful, he would get away, leaving her running to follow.

Vicky was sure Darien never noticed her plight as she struggled to keep up with the pace he set. Maybe he took a sadistic pleasure in seeing how far he could push his new little shadow before she complained about his breakneck speed? Now she understood what her contact at the temp agency had meant when they said her new boss was a difficult man to please. It would've been nice to have a little more warning about *whom* she was going to be interviewing with.

Setting her jaw in determination, Vicky dumped a brick of ramen noodles in a pot and added the water and spices. She wasn't going to complain about the job and be let go on the first day, as she needed this job if she was going to stay in Brenton. Vicky was currently down to her last few dollars, and if she didn't make this work out, she was going to have to go back to selling plasma to make up the rent on her tiny apartment.

Pulling the pin from her hair, Vicky headed into the bedroom to change out of her suit while her food cooked. She stripped from her work clothing in favor of some sweatpants and a T-shirt and was just heading back to the kitchen when she heard a strange noise. Looking around for the source of the eerie music, she realized that the phone Darien had given her was ringing. She caught it up and snapped it open.

"Hello?"

"I was starting to worry that you wouldn't answer." Darien's pleased voice rolled out of the phone.

"Sorry, the ring tone surprised me." Vicky said the first thing that came to her mind, smacking her head at how dumb she sounded when Darien snickered on the other end of the line.

16

"Bach's *Toccata and Fugue* in D minor. Such a lovely piece," he mused for a moment before turning to the reason he called. "Sorry to disturb you so soon after getting home, Miss Westernly, but I need something." Darien's voice took on a more serious tone.

"What can I do for you, Mr. Ritter?" Vicky went back to the kitchen and clicked off the gas under her dinner. It looked as if she was going to have to go back out.

"I need something from the bag. Can you please bring it to Fourth and Vine Street?"

That was just a couple of blocks down from where Vicky lived. "Let me change, and I'll be on my way." She started to head to the bedroom to put her work clothing back on, but Darien's words stopped her.

"I don't care what you're wearing; I need it now."

She grabbed some socks and changed her course for the door. "Yes, Mr. Ritter. I'm on my way."

Hanging up the phone, Vicky pulled her running shoes on over the socks and grabbed the messenger bag from the floor. Snagging a bandana for her hair, she hit the door at a run. The sadistic man had to be testing her, and she would be damned if she gave him a reason to fire her tonight.

Darien checked his watch as he waited for his new personal assistant to arrive. It had been about five minutes since she said she was on her way and hung up without waiting for a reply. He knew she lived close from her employment file and figured it would take her about thirty minutes to walk the distance. Leaning against the wall, he disappeared into the shadows of the night to wait. Darien liked watching how people, so accustomed to the light, handled darkness and the things it hid.

While studying a scantily clad woman trying to convince a very drunk man that she was worth the fifty bucks it would take to pick her up, Darien's attention was grabbed when something familiar shot past. Turning his eyes towards the streak, he found his assistant had arrived almost twenty minutes before he had expected her to.

Huffing, Vicky leaned against the lamppost on the corner where he had sent her and grasped at the stitch that had formed in her side from the run. She rubbed at it before standing up and looking around to find her new boss.

Darien clung to the shadows, studying her. He noted that Vicky's hair hung free about halfway down her back, held in place by a purple bandana that clashed with her neon green T-shirt and blue sweatpants. While looking around for the man who had called her out, she walked back and forth, stretching the lactic acid from her legs.

Darien watched for another minute until the hooker, having lost her mark, turned towards the young woman to see if she was horning in on her corner. When Vicky raised her hands to fend off the woman and stepped backwards, he emerged from the darkness, straight into the retreating woman's path so that she bumped into him. "Is there a problem, Miss Westernly?"

Vicky whirled around to see the man she was looking for and let out a sigh of relief. "Just a misunderstanding, Mr. Ritter." She stepped out of her boss's personal space.

Darien looked up to see the light in the hooker's eyes. She knew a man of money when she saw one, and she was going to do her best to make sure that this handsome guy took her home, not the scrawny thing in front of him.

"Hey, baby." She sashayed up to Darien. "I can show you a much better time than she can."

He looked down at the woman with curious eyes. "Can you now?" Darien asked in a sophisticated tone.

The woman smiled at him and stepped closer to play with his tie. Vicky moved back from the pair. She didn't know what was going to happen, but she suddenly felt the need to run.

"Of course I can," the working girl answered, before looking up at the burning, green eyes of her potential mark. Her hands froze on his tie as Darien released just a hint of power. The intense pressure staggered the offending woman back, and he smiled at her.

"I really don't think you can." Darien turned away and swallowed back the little bit of power that had been released, so he wouldn't frighten his new employee.

Vicky just stared at him, wide-eyed. She didn't know what she had just witnessed, but she was not going to ask and risk her meal ticket. "I b-b—" Vicky swallowed hard, trying to stop the stutter that had slipped into her voice, "—brought the bag for you, Mr. Ritter."

Darien sighed. He hadn't meant to scare his new assistant with his little demonstration. He was almost positive she wouldn't be showing up for work tomorrow. "Thank you," he sighed. There was nothing he could do about it now, short of erasing her memories, but he liked the girl and fiddling with people's minds had always given him problems. Everyone he had ever tried that trick on seemed a little flighty after he was done, if they remembered anything at all.

Vicky pulled the bag from where it hung on her hip and raised it, so Darien could get into it. He pulled out an electronic key fob before dropping the flap back into place. Vicky stared at the box in his hand in surprise. She had emptied out the satchel earlier and was sure it hadn't been in there.

Darien turned and started down the street. Vicky just stood there, trying to work out how she had missed that when she had done her exploration.

Darien paused in his retreat and turned back to the frozen woman. "Are you coming, Miss Westernly?"

Her feet moved automatically to join him. Vicky muttered an apology for her delay, and the pair walked slowly down the street.

The hooker stared after the girl with pity and crossed herself. She didn't know what the tall man was, but he terrified her. The look he had given her spoke of death and destruction, and she actually feared for the safety of the young woman walking away with him.

Vicky walked next to her employer as they headed in the opposite direction of her home. She glanced back over her shoulder, wondering if Darien needed her to stay or if she was free to go back to her apartment now. Her stomach chose that moment to remind her she hadn't eaten since the half-finished sandwich at noon.

Darien smiled at the sound and turned his attention to his young companion. "Have you had dinner yet?" he asked softly.

Vicky looked up at his profile before returning her attention to the darkened street in front of her. "Not yet," she admitted. "I was in the process of making something when you called."

"I'm sorry I pulled you away," Darien replied. "Will it be okay?" He was genuinely concerned for the girl. The lunch she had at work seemed rather pathetic. He imagined she was hungry.

"It'll be fine." She waved his worry away. "It's only ramen."

Darien cocked an eyebrow at her. He had run her hard today, and she was only having ramen noodles for dinner? This would not do at all. He stopped next to a black sports car and opened the passenger door with the fob from Vicky's bag.

She looked questionably at the expensive, little two-seater and then at her boss, trying to decide if she really wanted to be trapped in a small space with the powerful man. Seeing no way to refuse without losing her job, she climbed into the passenger seat.

Darien laughed silently as he walked around to the other side of the car and got in. He liked that she was wary of him. It meant she knew danger when she saw it, and that was always a good instinct to have.

Pulling the Aston Martin DB9 into light traffic, Darien took off faster than he really should have. Vicky gripped the handle of the door as he slipped the car into spaces almost too small for it to go. She had never been in anything this powerful... or expensive.

She assumed he was giving her a ride home, but they zipped past her building without even slowing down. Staring out the window, Vicky tried to make sense of what was happening. "Where are we going?" she finally asked.

"To get something to eat," Darien answered as he pulled up to a red light.

Vicky gave him a confused look. "I've got dinner waiting at home," she informed him again, in case he hadn't heard the first time.

"I know, but your noodles will probably be very

soggy by the time you get back," he explained. "Consider this an apology for getting you out so late and ruining your meal."

Vicky thought about refusing the offer, but the man was right. By the time she got back, the noodles would be mushy and unpleasant. "That's very kind of you, Mr. Ritter," she thanked him.

An odd grin curled the edges of Darien's mouth. It had been some time since anyone had sincerely told him he was kind.

Pulling the sports car up to the curb, Darien shut it off.

Vicky looked out the window at the darkened building next to her. This was the rich end of town, and she knew of no place around here that would allow her inside dressed as she was. Darien opened the door, and she stared out at him. He cocked his head in question, and she stepped out, clutching the bag to her.

Shutting the car door behind her, he led the way across the street into a low-lit doorway. Following her boss, Vicky's steps faltered before hitting the mat in front of the restaurant that was clearly an upper-class establishment.

Darien paused as he noticed her hesitation. "Is there something wrong?" He looked back to the door he was holding open for the reluctant woman. "Do you not like Japanese?"

Vicky shook her head, trying to hide behind the messenger bag. "That's not it, Mr. Ritter," she explained. "I'm not dressed for someplace like this." Vicky felt her boss's eyes travel over her as if he were seeing her for the first time.

"You're right."

She sighed in relief as Darien conceded her point and released the door. Now, she just had to convince him to get her a quick hamburger and let her go home. Before she knew what happened, Darien had his hand on her shoulder and was propelling her into the shop next to the restaurant. He spoke in quick Japanese to the shopkeeper. Vicky didn't even have a chance to voice her protest before she was relieved of her bag and pushed into the waiting hands of a small woman.

Twenty minutes later, Vicky was let out of the building in the most beautiful kimono she had ever seen. Her outfit was completed with Zori sandals over Tabi socks, a small bag that matched the obi, and a dark, wooden comb placed smartly in her hair. Her T-shirt, shoes, and pants had been stuck in a wooden box and given to the shop owner with instructions that Vicky didn't dream of understanding.

"That's better," Darien said as he looked over the outfit his assistant was decked out in. The silk of the kimono started a soft, silvery blue around the collar and shifted in intensity as it fell away from Vicky's shoulders, so the ends of the sleeves and hem were the blue of a clear sky. There were curvy branches of golds and grays hand painted on the sleeves and down the length of the garment. The kimono was held in place by a peach-colored, textured-silk obi with some kind of large, reddish flowers on a light brown branch and a cord the same color as the deepest blue of the kimono. Vicky felt odd, swaddled in such unusual clothing, but Darien nodded his approval and tucked her hand into his arm as he led her back to the door of the Japanese restaurant.

The houseman welcomed Darien with a warm smile

and a greeting that Vicky recognized from the numerous ninja movies she had watched with her friends in college. The two men spoke for a minute before Darien and Vicky were escorted to a table. This restaurant catered to a wide range of clientele, and Darien thought it would be best to arrange for a Western-style table. He didn't think Vicky would be able to handle sitting on the floor in her lovely, new outfit.

As it was, she sat gingerly on the edge of her chair so as not to crush the massive folds of material tied to her back. She hadn't seen what that lady put back there, but she felt as if she had a pillow tied to her butt.

Darien set the messenger bag down by his feet and joined his companion at the table. He spoke rapidly to the waiter, and the man left without showing them the menus.

Vicky sat silently through the entire exchange, not knowing what to say or if the waiter would even understand her. "I thought we were getting dinner?" she asked, as she watched the menus leave without being opened.

An amused grin curled the corners of Darien's lips. "It'll be out in a few minutes."

"Oh." Vicky folded her hands in her lap and studied the weave of the tablecloth. She had no idea what was going on, but she could feel the eyes of her new boss boring into her from across the table. Gathering up her courage, Vicky looked up into those emerald green orbs. Her mouth went dry at the way the man's eyes sparkled like jewels in the dim light of the restaurant. The way he stared at her made Vicky feel like a little mouse cornered by a cat. And not just some little house cat, but one of those big felines that stared out from the top of cliffs, unseen, before springing out to rip the throat from unsuspecting prey.

"So, Miss Westernly, tell me about yourself." Darien leaned forward in his chair, placing his elbows on the table as he spoke. His fingers laced together, and he rested his hands on the table in front of him as he waited for his assistant to answer.

Vicky picked up the water glass and took a sip to lubricate her throat, so her voice wouldn't crack when she spoke. "What would you like to know?" she asked, unsure what her boss wanted to hear. She was worried she would say something wrong, and he would dismiss her services.

"I would like to know whom the woman I'm entrusting my life to really is," Darien explained.

Vicky's mind whirled on this thought. She never expected Darien Ritter would want to know anything about her. "Well, I don't know where to start," she admitted. "I grew up just outside of the small town of Moraine, the only child of Thomas and Ann Westernly." She felt that her background was insignificant, but the great man employing her had asked. "Daddy was a farmer until he was killed by a drunk driver when I was fourteen. After he died, Mom sold the farm, and we moved into town so that she could be closer to her job." Vicky continued to recount her simple life, up to the point when she moved to Brenton on her mother's claim that Vicky would have better employment opportunities in the city. When finished, she fell silent and waited for some response from the man watching her.

Darien had listened intently to Vicky's story without comment and now considered the life that had been laid out before him. Other than the death of her father and the sale of her childhood home, this woman had lived a fairly normal, quiet life. Having watched her face closely, he'd tracked the emotions that played across her eyes as she spoke. He could tell that she still felt pain at the loss of the man who had raised her, and love for the mother who urged her to better herself. It was also apparent that she had started to relax as she spoke, but now she was starting to tense back up as she waited for him to judge her. Darien withdrew his hands from the table and leaned back in his chair. "What made you choose a degree in business?" he asked.

Vicky was surprised Darien hadn't made any comment about her provincial life. Picking up the new topic to dispel her growing tension, she talked about job availability and wages, but nothing that would suggest a desire to work in the business world. Only that it was a secure future her mother had pushed her towards as she looked into colleges.

Vicky had been avoiding looking at Darien's face as she spoke—his eyes made her uneasy—but she glanced up as she rambled on and fell silent at the look she found there. She could tell that he was slightly disappointed with her answer. Picking up her water glass to cover the pause in conversation, she tried to think of a way to save her job.

Setting the drink down, she prepared to continue her answer when the waiter appeared with two little bottles, some small cups, and a bowl of bean pods. Darien thanked him and reached for the pods. Vicky watched curiously as her boss popped the pod open and slipped the first of the beans into his mouth.

He looked up to find her watching him and liked how the girl's emotions rode her face. It made it easy for him to see what she was thinking. "Have you ever had edamame before?"

Vicky shook her head, and he pushed the bowl of green pods closer so she could reach them without dragging her sleeves across the table.

He took another pod and split it along the seam. "You eat just the beans inside," Darien showed her the small, green pieces.

She picked one of the beans up and broke it open with her nail. It looked vaguely familiar, and she rolled it between her fingers before putting the slightly salty legume into her mouth. Inspecting the pod and its damp, slightly fuzzy skin, Vicky remembered where she had seen this vegetable before. "Are these soybeans?" she asked.

Darien smiled and confirmed her guess. Picking up one of the little bottles, he poured some of the clear liquid into one of the cups.

Now that he was no longer just staring at her, Vicky felt more at ease. She picked up the little cup to see what Darien had offered. Raising it to her lips, she took a swallow. The cool liquid ran across her tongue and down her throat like a good wine should. She never had sake before and was unsure what to expect from the drink. Taking another taste, she relished the drink before setting the dish back on the table. The two sips had almost drained the small vessel, and Darien refilled it for her. She thanked him but didn't pick it up again. Vicky hadn't eaten much today and knew drinking on an empty stomach could lead to some very awkward situations, especially with a new boss whom she was trying hard not to disappoint.

She was saved from commenting about the food

when the waiter brought out a large, steaming bowl and placed it on the table in front of her. Vicky looked into the dish and almost laughed out loud. She couldn't keep the smile off her face as she questioned her boss's choice of food. "Ramen noodles?"

"You said you were going to have ramen for dinner," Darien's eyes twinkled mischievously as he spoke. "It just seemed right."

Vicky couldn't stop the giggle that slipped from her.

The delicate sound surprised Darien, and he smiled as she picked up the bowl and blew on the hot liquid. She sipped some of the broth from the noodles and set the bowl back on the table to pick up the chopsticks. Darien watched her with half-lidded eyes as he sipped on a cup of sake.

"Aren't you eating?" Vicky asked, noticing the lack of food in front of her host.

He shook his head. "I've already eaten tonight." He left out the fact that his dinner had been very different from her delicious-smelling repast.

Vicky suddenly felt strange eating while her boss watched, but she took comfort in the fact that he munched on the bowl of edamame. She ate her noodles and drank several more cups of the rice wine under Darien's watchful eyes. No longer feeling like prey being stalked, she now felt like a bug in a glass jar under a magnifying glass. She just hoped that he didn't see anything that would make him change his mind about hiring her.

When she was done, the waiter came and took the empty bowl away. Darien paid the bill with one of the credit cards from the bag at his feet. "So, how was it?" He stood up to leave.

"Those were the best ramen noodles I've ever had," Vicky admitted, as her boss led the way to the door.

Darien laughed at her response.

She looked back at his seat and saw he had forgotten the messenger bag. Retrieving it by the handle on top, she hurried to catch up to him. She didn't want to sling the strap over her shoulder and ruin the beautiful kimono. As she stepped out of the restaurant, Vicky expected Darien to turn to return the clothing she had borrowed, but her boss headed straight to the black sports car they arrived in. She stopped on the sidewalk, shocked, and looked at the shop where her clothing had been left.

Darien turned when she didn't come and followed her eyes to the little store. "Come on," Darien called. Vicky's feet moved towards him automatically. "Don't worry about your clothes. They'll be delivered to the office tomorrow."

Her mouth fell open as she realized that he had no intention of returning the silk robes wrapped around her.

As he held the car door for her, Vicky settled into the passenger seat, muttering softly. Darien smiled when he saw she'd picked up the bag he'd left behind. Glad the spell on the satchel had settled on Vicky so quickly, he was sure she wouldn't be able to lose it now. The bag was enchanted, so whomever Darien gave it to would want to keep it with them, and others wouldn't be willing to pick it up. After all, it did have his entire life hidden within its folds.

"Dreaming. Yes, that's it—I'm dreaming," Darien heard Vicky mutter, as she sat on the edge of the seat with the satchel in her lap.

"What do you mean 'dreaming'?" he asked, starting

the car and pointing it back toward Vicky's apartment building.

"That's the only thing I can come up with to explain tonight." She spoke a little louder as Darien looked sideways at her. "Stuff like this just doesn't happen in real life, so I must be dreaming."

He grinned at her logic.

"That explains the thing with the hooker, the key that shouldn't have been in the bag, and buying a kimono to have ramen noodle soup." Vicky rambled on, convincing herself that she had fallen asleep on the couch when she had first come home.

Darien chuckled at her. It was obvious she was feeling the sake as he pulled up in front of her apartment building. He opened her door, and she swayed a little as she tried to stand. Darien caught her in his arms before she could fall to the sidewalk. He took the leather bag from her and slung it over his shoulder to help her up the steps to her apartment.

Vicky pulled her keys from the little bag that matched her outfit and leaned on her new boss as she worked the door open. She stumbled inside when the door swung free, but Darien stopped before he crossed the threshold of her home.

"May I come in?"

Vicky turned back to see Darien had stopped at the door. "Sure." She swayed, surprised by how polite the eccentric man was being. "Please, come in."

Darien could feel the power that held him out give way as he stepped across the threshold and into the small apartment. He dropped the satchel on the sofa and took Vicky back into his arms before she fell.

Her breath hitched as he pulled her closer. That

little gasp of air filled her with his rich, spicy smell. It had a slightly coppery tang that she had never experienced with anyone else, but it was far from unpleasant. She found it almost as intoxicating as the sake she had consumed with dinner. His skin was cooler than she had imagined, but the muscles she could feel under his tailored suit were just as hard as she had expected. Vicky squeaked slightly as he lifted her from her feet and carried her across the room and through the door leading to her bedroom.

Darien placed her on her feet and proceeded to start stripping off the exotic clothing he was sure she wouldn't be able to remove on her own.

Vicky pushed his hands away. "I'm not that type of a girl," she squeaked, as she tried to back away from the man she thought was trying to take advantage of her drunken state.

Darien chuckled. It had been a while since a woman had pushed him away while he was undressing her. It was rather refreshing. "I'm sorry," he apologized. "I was only trying to help you with the unfamiliar clothing."

Vicky eyed him, warily crossing her arms over her chest protectively. She knew how dangerous it was to have a strange man in her bedroom, and she never meant for him to get this far into her apartment.

Darien could see she wasn't going to let him help without some kind of persuasion. He thought about just slipping into her thoughts and pressing her to his will, but that could lead to some odd tensions if she continued to work for him. He thought back to her drunken ramblings in the car. "You're dreaming all of this, right?" Darien raised an eyebrow at the defensive girl.

Vicky froze. "Have to be," she responded. She was

98% certain that what had happened tonight couldn't be real.

"Then there's no problem if I help you with the kimono," Darien coaxed her into relenting. "It's just a dream, after all."

Vicky relaxed a little as he reached out to pull her towards him. He loosened the ends of the cord holding her obi in place. "It's just a dream," he said again, softly, as Vicky calmed.

She stood perfectly still as he pulled the wide strip of cloth from around her and set it on the foot of the bed. He slipped the waistband beneath the obi off, letting the outer kimono fall loose around her. Spinning her around, he pulled the silken robes from her body and laid them on top of the obi. Gently reminding her that this was still a dream, he turned her so he could relieve her of the under kimono in the same fashion.

When she stood in just the undershirt and half-slip worn under the outer garments, Darien stopped undressing his new assistant and turned her around again. She moved willingly under his hands as he propelled her to the edge of her bed. "It's only a dream," Darien whispered again, pulling back the covers to place Vicky in bed. Slipping the sandals from her feet, he reached up to pull the comb from her hair. He could hear her heartbeat increase and her breathing stop as he ran his fingers through her dark blonde locks, checking for any bobby pins that might have been used to help hold the soft hair in place. Darien forced her to swing her legs up and into the bedding. He could see a slight hint of fear in Vicky's eyes, as he made sure she was properly placed in the bed. The fear subsided when he covered her up instead of climbing in with her.

Darien set the delicate comb on the nightstand and checked the alarm clock to make sure it would wake Vicky up in the morning. He reached out and patted her on the head, lightly, like a child. "Sleep well, and don't be late for work tomorrow."

"Thank you," Vicky called to the retreating form of her new boss before closing her eyes and letting sleep take her away. She was sure she would wake up tomorrow morning on the couch, still dressed in the suit she had worn to work that day.

Darien smiled warmly at the woman snuggled in the covers before he shut the door to her room. He was glad the temp agency had sent her. Not only had she proven she could take what he could dish out at work, she delighted him with her innocence and ability to deal with the unexpected. And she hadn't complained once. Darien looked around Vicky's apartment as he let himself out. He approved of her home. It was small, but clean and pleasant, and it fit her personality well.

Stepping out into the night air, he breathed deeply. It was still early, and he suddenly felt the need for something warmer than the drawn blood he had consumed earlier. Maybe he could find the working girl that was so eager earlier and 'convince' her to donate a pint.

Standing in front of her boss's partially opened door, Vicky wavered, not sure if she should let him know she was there. She was a little apprehensive about facing him after waking up to find the magnificent kimono draped across the foot of her bed. In the crisp light of the morning, she had to finally admit that what had happened last night was not a dream. She had spent most of the morning reprimanding herself, and she half-expected Darien to send her home for being unprofessional. Looking back at her desk, she almost decided to sit down and wait for her new boss to come find her. Shaking off this idea, she plucked up her courage and knocked on the expensive, wooden door, but got no answer.

"Mr. Ritter," she called, in case he had missed the soft knock. When no answer came, Vicky pushed the door open just a little and poked her head in. Finding the room void of its occupant, she swung the door open fully and stepped into her boss's office. Seeing she was safe for a few more minutes, she approached Darien's neat desk and dropped the present she had brought in the middle. She turned to find her employer standing in the doorway with a cup of coffee and a newspaper. Vicky blushed at being caught in his office. "Good morning, Mr. Ritter." Her voice came out a little quicker than intended as she tucked her hands behind her back. She felt like a kid getting caught in a cookie jar.

Darien raised an eyebrow at the unexpected presence of his assistant in his office. "Good morning, Miss Westernly." He leaned a little to see what she had done to his desk, but she was standing too close for him to see around her. Straightening back up, he focused on the woman working for him. The corner of his mouth curled up as he took in the loose, knee-length skirt and low-heeled pumps that would be easy to move in. She was ready for another day like yesterday. "I trust you slept well."

The color on her skin deepened as she remembered how she got to bed. "Yes. Thank you for taking care of me." Vicky tried to find a way past the man filling the doorway.

"You're welcome," he answered, as if it had just been another normal night.

This calmed Vicky a bit. Since he hadn't made a big deal out of it, she stood a good chance of keeping her job. Her heart jumped as Darien walked into the room, angling his course so he could get around the desk. She swallowed down her fear and embarrassment and stood her ground as he moved. It wouldn't do her any good to bolt from the room like a startled rabbit. "If there is anything I can do, please let me know," she offered, turning to go.

Darien stopped when his eyes fell on the two little fruits. He moved around behind his desk and called to her before she could reach the door. "What's this?"

She turned to see what her boss was looking at. She knew the answer, but it would only be proper to face him when she spoke. "They're clementines," she said.

Darien chuckled lightly. "I know that. What are they doing on my desk?" He pinned Vicky with a sharp look.

She shifted from foot to foot as she answered, "I, um..." she started, and then rephrased her thoughts. "You liked the one from yesterday so much, I thought you would like a few more."

Darien closed his eyes and smiled gently. The simple gesture warmed his heart, and he looked back at the girl waiting for him to respond. "Thank you." Darien dropped the newspaper on his desk and picked up one of the little oranges to give it a light squeeze. He could smell the fresh tang of the rind as the oils released under his fingers.

Vicky nodded her head and left the office, pulling the door shut.

He tossed the clementine up and caught it before lifting it to his nose to breathe in its rich scent. It did more to liven his senses than the coffees he had taken to drinking.

Sitting down in his chair, Darien pushed his drink away to look over the morning paper. His eyes took in the dreadful headline over the picture of the charred building that had once been a home. "Body Count Rises in Southside Slaughters." He perused the article to see that three more people had met horrible ends at the hands of some unknown assailant. Two bodies had been burnt beyond recognition, and one had been torn to little bits and scattered across the yard of the burnt home. This brought the body count to nine.

There had only been four fires, but every event had

left at least one person reduced to palm-sized chunks. The police had no witnesses and no idea as to who was responsible. The few people that were able to help could only confirm that the fires went from nothing to full-blown in a matter of minutes, but no one had been able to tell how the bodies had been ground up. This entire thing had the smell of something supernatural, but as long as it stayed away from his world, Darien didn't want to get involved. He shook his head and flipped the paper to the business section. Laying it across his desk, he tore into the fruit he had been playing with.

Vicky looked at the time on her computer to find that Darien's first appointment should be arriving soon. She stood up to knock on her boss's door. "Your first appointment will be here in about ten minutes," she informed him before her eyes fell to the massacre on the desk.

He had absentmindedly shredded the peel of one of the clementines all over his desktop as he read through his morning paper. There wasn't a single piece bigger than the nail on her pinky. Vicky nearly laughed as Darien looked at the mess, slightly surprised. It was like he had no idea how the rind had fragmented itself. The oil from the peel had colored his fingers yellow, and Vicky giggled at him. "Go wash your hands and I'll clean this up," she said as she walked towards the desk. Darien thanked her and disappeared out the office door to wash up. She folded the newspaper and swiped the pieces of peel into the trashcan.

"Do you see anything else?" Darien asked when he came back from the restroom. He looked over the desk that Vicky had made presentable again. She had even picked up the pieces of peel that had fallen to the floor by his chair.

She glanced over the room, and then up to her boss. "Fix your tie." Vicky pointed out the only imperfection she could see.

Darien looked at her, confused, and then studied his image reflected in the tinted office window. "What?" he asked, unable to see anything wrong with his tie.

"The knot at the top is lopsided."

Darien stepped closer to the reflective surface and looked again. It was the same as it always was. He wiggled it a little to straighten it and turned back to his assistant.

She shook her head signaling that it wasn't right. "It's the knot you used. Those are really hard to get straight." She held her hands out, asking if she could fix it. "May I?"

"Please." Darien stood up straight to let her work. This was the same knot he had been using since bowties had gone out of style.

Vicky took a deep breath and stepped into Darien's personal space. Pulling his tie off, she flipped it over and proceeded to twist the ends around into a neat, Shelby knot. She pushed it up into place and patted his collar down over the band. Before stepping away, she fiddled with it for another moment, and then nodded her satisfaction.

Darien turned to look at his reflection and was surprised at how much of a change the different style of knot made. "Where did you learn that?"

"I learned it from my uncle when I was little and got good at it in college." Vicky glanced away from her boss as she spoke. "One of the guys I dated could never get his tie straight, so he had me fix it for him."

He let out a light laugh. "You'll have to teach me

how it's done later."

Vicky smiled and excused herself to go back out and wait for his appointment.

Darien looked at his reflection in the glass again and grinned. That girl was just full of surprises.

❖❖◗O◖❖❖

Vicky kicked her shoes off and dropped her bag on the couch in her apartment. Today had been another busy day, but nowhere near as crazy as yesterday. She had been ready to chase after Darien with her new voice recorder and more comfortable shoes, but the man seemed to take his time with everything today. She even had to prod him along so he would make it to his appointments on time. It boggled her mind how her boss could be so hectic one day and so relaxed the next. Was he messing with her? Pushing the thought away, Vicky pulled the wooden kimono box from her bag and took it to the bedroom so she could properly care for the beautiful robe from last night.

The sound of Vicky's normal cell phone interrupted her as she pulled the silken fabric into place. She retrieved it and smiled at the name showing on the caller ID.

"Hey, Vanessa," Vicky called down the line to her best friend. "What's happening?" She was rewarded with a hardy laugh from the speaker.

"Not much. Just calling to see how you're doing." Vicky and Vanessa had been roommates in college and had grown close in the four years they spent together.

"Doing pretty good," Vicky confessed. "I finally got a decent job."

"Oh, yeah?" Vicky could hear the curious note in Vanessa's voice. "It's not like that last one, is it?"

Vicky shuddered as she remembered her previous

job and the smelly, little man who invaded her personal space every time he saw her. He creeped her out so badly that she dreaded going to work. "Nothing like that. This boss may be a little more eccentric," Vicky glanced at the kimono stretched out on her bed, "but he's definitely better to work with."

"That's good. Did you hear about the fire last night?" Vanessa changed the subject to the reason she called.

"You mean the latest in the 'Southside Slaughter' case?" Vicky had scanned over the headlines briefly while cleaning the mess from Darien's desk this morning.

"Yeah, that's the one. That was Becka's house."

Vicky stood in shock as she took in this news. "You don't mean Rebecca and Charlie, do you?" Vanessa made a positive noise, and Vicky had to sit down before she fell. "Are you sure?" Her mind flew over what little of the article she had read to see if she could remember if the victims' names had been given.

"I recognized it from the picture in the paper," Vanessa sighed. "I was over there a few weeks ago to go shopping with her. She was four months pregnant."

Vicky's heart clenched at hearing this news. Rebecca was more Vanessa's friend then hers, but they had all hung out at college. "That's horrible," Vicky couldn't believe what her friend was telling her. "That makes four people I knew who have been killed by this crazy arsonist." She hugged herself as a chill ran down her back.

"*Four?*" Vanessa exclaimed. "Who were the other two?"

"Samantha Bridge and Carla Michaels. They were both in my creative writing class."

Vanessa whistled. "That's scary. Marsha Thompson was in my business ethics class." She fell quiet on the phone for a moment. "Between the two of us, we know five of the victims. I wonder if we'll know the other four once they're identified."

"I don't think I'm going to sleep well until they catch this guy," Vicky told her friend.

"You're safe," Vanessa laughed at her. "He's only hit single-family homes on the south side of town. I doubt he would try this shit on an apartment complex in the east. Now me, I'm a different matter. I live on the south side."

"Don't say those kinds of things, Vanessa," Vicky scolded. "If we knew everyone, there's a possibility we could be the next targets. You want to come over and stay for a while till this thing blows over?"

"Nah, I just had the smoke detectors in my house checked and bought a fire extinguisher to put under my bedside table," Vanessa reassured her. "I should be fine."

Vicky nodded her approval. "Good."

"Hey, we're getting together this weekend to go clubbing. You coming?"

Vicky smirked at how fast Vanessa could go from grisly fires to the dorm girls' monthly hangout. "Sure. Same place as always?"

"Yup."

"Cool. Unless something comes up, I'll be there at eight, like normal," Vicky said with a smile.

"Great! I'll let the other girls know you're coming. We can celebrate your new job. I've got to run now, so we'll see you Saturday."

Vicky said farewell to her friend and hung up. She stood and turned to face the garment laying across her bed. Now, if she could just remember how that website had said to fold the thing up, she could get it in the wooden box where it belonged.

4

Vicky clicked her way across the website of the local bookstore, looking for something that would help her with her plight. She had spent an hour last night trying to get the kimono folded correctly, but it never looked like the pictures on the website. She finally gave up and fed the handle of a broom through the sleeves, tacking it to the wall with a few lengths of yarn and some pushpins. It wasn't the suggested way to store the amazing garment, but at least it got it up off the bed so she could sleep.

Finally, she chose an available book that looked promising and ordered it for pick up. She looked up at the clock to find that it was almost four. It would probably be safe to go home at five.

Most of the day had been spent sitting at her desk, learning about kimonos and their history. Darien was nowhere to be found this morning when Vicky arrived at seven. It wasn't until she called the answering service to get his messages that she finally heard from her elusive boss. The message he'd left didn't explain much, just that he wouldn't be in this morning, and that she should cancel and reschedule his meetings for the day.

Surprisingly, this hadn't been difficult, and she was left twiddling her thumbs after nine. She did go down to chat with Sue at lunchtime, but she came back to her desk right away, worried that she would get in trouble for not being in the office during the day.

Vicky sighed as she hit a bomb on what had to be her hundredth game of Minesweeper since she started playing after lunch. She wondered if it would be okay to download that game where you fought off zombies by planting flowers in the yard. It was cute and would be fun on days when she had nothing to do, but she decided to put it off until she could feel out her boss a little bit more. Yes, he had told her she could do whatever she wanted in her down time, but loading games onto the company laptop might be a little too tacky for the first week on the job.

Vicky clicked the restart button and had just started popping little flags across the grid when the door to the outer office banged open, startling her. She looked up to find that her boss had finally shown up, carrying two large boxes stacked together. Jumping up, she rushed to relieve him of the top one so he could see where he was going.

"Thank you," Darien said, and stopped to look at the girl he hadn't expected to see. "What are you still doing here?" he asked as he led the way to her desk to put the heavy boxes down.

"I wasn't sure what to do when you didn't come in," she confessed. "I got the message and rescheduled your appointments, but I didn't know if I should stay or not."

Darien grinned at her. "So you hung around here all day with nothing to do?"

She nodded.

"That is very responsible, Miss Westernly. Next time I have you cancel everything and you have nothing to do, you can leave. If you're still unsure, call and ask. You have my cell phone number."

Vicky blushed at her foolishness. Of course she should have called him.

Darien dropped his box on the floor next to Vicky's desk and moved so she could add her box to it. He knelt down to pull one of the tops off, showing the stacks of paper jammed inside. "These are from a business that I'm considering backing. This is all of their financial information for the last two years, but it's a bit of a mess. I want it put into a spreadsheet, so I can see if this will be a good investment or not. I was going to leave it till tomorrow, but since you're already here, could you sort it out?"

Vicky's eyes widened as she took in how much work her boss had just dropped on her. Did he expect her to do it all tonight?

Looking up at his silent secretary, he chuckled at the surprise on her face. "I need it by the end of the month."

She let out a sigh of relief. As long as she had a little time to work on it, there wouldn't be a problem. "Sure thing, Mr. Ritter," Vicky agreed to the monumental task.

Darien dropped the lid back onto the box and stood up. "If you need anything, just let me know." He turned towards his office as she looked down at the two boxes, thinking about the best way to tackle this project. "Thank you, Miss Westernly," he called from the doorway before disappearing inside.

Vicky sighed. At least he was polite about ruining her plans to leave early. She checked the clock. If she hurried, she could make it down to the supply office for some manila folders before they cut out for the evening.

Vicky looked up from the stack of papers she was sorting through to check the time. Ten o'clock AM. Her crazy boss hadn't shown up again this morning, but there had been no message about canceling his day. There was only an hour until his next appointment, and if she had read the book correctly, this one was across town. Fearing Darien had forgotten about it, Vicky set the papers on her desk and fished out the cell phone to call him. He picked up on the second ring.

"What can I do for you, Miss Westernly?" Darien's voice crackled through the line. The reception was really bad.

"I was just calling to remind you about the appointment this morning with Mr. Rodgers." Vicky held the phone away from her ear, trying to save herself from the horrible static.

"Can you drive a standard?"

She was surprised by his question. "Yes."

"Good. Call Mr. Rodgers and tell him we'll be about an hour late. Take the elevator to the basement garage, ask Charlie in the guardhouse for the keys to my car, and come pick me up. I'll be landing at Hawking's Field in about forty-five minutes. Understand?"

Vicky confirmed his instructions before hanging up and scrambling to collect the files spread across the floor. Hawking's Field was a tiny airfield on the outskirts of the city, and if she didn't hurry she wouldn't make it in time.

With her ever-present messenger bag slung over

her shoulder, Vicky stepped off the elevator into the building's underground parking garage. Until Darien told her about it, she didn't even know this floor existed. She looked around, found the little guardhouse, and knocked on the door. An elderly man who reminded Vicky of her grandfather greeted her. "I'm Victoria Westernly, and I was sent to get Mr. Ritter's car," she explained.

The man smiled at her and pulled a key from a pegboard behind him. He made Vicky sign his log before handing over the key. "You'll find her in Bay 465. She's all ready for you, but please be careful." Charlie pointed her in the direction of the car she was going to take.

Vicky thanked him and promised to be careful before heading on her way. The layout of the garage was interesting. On one side were normal parking places with a random assortment of vehicles ranging from shipping trucks to some very high-class sports cars. Vicky's eyes found the Aston Martin that Darien had taken her to dinner in parked among these cars. On the other side were a series of enclosed bays. Each bay was twice as wide as a normal parking place and had a roll-up door that concealed and protected whatever was inside. Vicky counted the bays as she searched for the one she wanted. She couldn't help but wonder what Darien had hidden behind all those doors.

She soon found out when she came to Bay 465. The door was up, and the light came on as soon as she stepped inside. Vicky gasped at the cherry-red finish of the 1957 Ford Fairlane Skyliner waiting for her. Charlie had already opened the windows and put the top down. She had only seen pictures of the hardtop convertible, but it had always been a favorite of her father's. A tear came to her eye as she thought about what her daddy would've said if he had known his little girl would get the chance to drive one.

Vicky carefully dropped her bag into the back seat and pulled the door open to get in. A smile split her face as the V8 purred to life, and she carefully pulled the car out of the bay. She waved at Charlie as she passed the guard-shack on her way out. The sun was shining warmly as she headed out to pick up her boss. This was going to be a fun drive.

Vicky pulled into the small airfield a few minutes before she was expected. The traffic had been light, and she had made good time. Parking the Skyliner near the main office, she checked her hair in the mirror. The pin she had used to hold it in place had come out when she hit the interstate, and the wind had done a number on her long locks. Lacking a brush to reset her hair, she pulled her fingers through it to ease most of the tangles out.

Once presentable again, Vicky went into the office to check if her boss had arrived yet. "Good morning," she greeted the woman in the office. "I'm here to pick up Mr. Ritter. Has he arrived yet?"

The young woman considered Vicky for a moment before smiling at her. "Not yet, but his plane is due in at any time. Just follow this road down to the end of the field and park on the left, inside the hanger." The woman pointed to the drive that passed in front of the building.

Vicky thanked her and went to wait for her boss.

Leaning against the side of the car, Vicky waited for Darien to arrive. She watched as the ground crew guided the plane into the building and cracked the hull open. She smiled as her tall boss emerged and looked around. There was a bit of a bounce in his step as he climbed from the plane and moved towards her.

"The café au lait is probably cold, but the beignets should be okay." Darien held out a brown bag and a cup of coffee for Vicky to take.

She gave him a confused look as she relieved him of the gift. Expecting him to get into the driver seat, he surprised her again by heading around and hopping into the passenger's side. Vicky took a sip of the chicory coffee laced with milk as she stowed the bag of beignets in the back with her satchel. The coffee had cooled off, but it was still tasty.

She slid into the driver's seat and looked over at the man who had relaxed back into his seat as if he were going to take a nap. "Are we going straight over to your meeting, or do you need to stop someplace first?" Vicky was unsure if this was the same suit her boss had worn yesterday or not.

Darien rolled his head a little and cracked an eye to look at her. "Straight over."

Vicky gave him a hearty "Yes, Mr. Ritter," and started the car.

Darien made a pained noise as soon as they pulled out of the hanger into the sunshine. "Could you please put the top up?"

She looked over in concern. Figuring he must have a hangover, Vicky quickly located the button that worked the roof.

He let out a relieved sigh as the top closed overhead, blocking out the sun. He hadn't realized it had gotten that late in the morning. Once more protected from the strong rays of the noonday sun, Darien relaxed back into the seat to enjoy the ride.

"Where'd you get the café au lait and beignets?" Vicky asked, sipping at her coffee.

"Café Du Monde." Darien smiled as if he was remembering something good.

Her brow furrowed, and she turned the cup to read the green logo on it. "You mean the one in *New Orleans*?" Vicky had heard of the famous shop but had never had a chance to see it.

"That's the one."

"*What* were you doing in New Orleans?" Vicky was too shocked that he had flown down there to stop the question from slipping from her mouth.

A mischievous grin curled the corners of her boss's mouth, and the tip of his tongue darted out to wet his lips. "I had a late night meeting with a Cajun."

Vicky's eyes widened at his answer, and she turned her mind to not wrecking the car. What her boss did on his own time was his own business, and she was not about to ask any more questions. She decided she should just do her job and shut the hell up.

After the last few days, Vicky wasn't sure what to expect from her eccentric boss. She was just glad it was finally Friday, and she only had one more day until she could relax and attempt to process the past week.

When she knocked on Darien's office door, she was surprised to find him already inside, poring over some files. "Good morning, Mr. Ritter. Please let me know if you need anything." Vicky dropped two clementines on his desk. She wanted to give him something nice for yesterday's beignets.

A look of amusement crossed Darien's face as he

looked over his papers at the gift. "Thank you very much, Miss Westernly."

Vicky nodded, and considered her boss. "You need to fix your tie." She pointed to the crooked knot at his throat. It was one of her pet peeves. Vicky was surprised when Darien dropped his paperwork to the desk and stood up.

He pulled off the strip of cloth as he rounded the desk and held it out to her. "Show me how to do it."

Vicky took the silk tie from Darien's hand. She quickly wrapped the material around her neck and demonstrated the knot she had learned. Darien watched her closely as she repeated it several times before handing the tie back.

He attempted to copy her movements but fumbled and ended up with the back of his tie facing outward.

Vicky giggled and stepped closer so she could help. "Like this." She flipped the fabric over to get him started.

Darien could hear Vicky's heartbeat quicken as she explained each step of the knot.

Once it was finished, she slid it into place and made sure his collar was neat before stepping back from the handsome man employing her. The way her heart pounded when they were close told her it was a bad idea to get physically near him. It would be too easy for Darien to sweep her away.

"Thank you." Darien, smiling warmly, looked down at Vicky.

Color bloomed on her cheeks as she excused herself from his office.

He watched Vicky go before returning to his desk and the work waiting for him. This was definitely the girl he needed to make sure his life ran smoothly. He made a note to call the temp agency and have her contract changed from a trial temp to a permanent hire.

5

THE HEAVY BEAT OF THE MUSIC PULSED THROUGH VICKY AS SHE glanced around the club for her friends. Finally laying eyes on the girls chatting in the corner, Vicky slipped through the growing crowd to their booth.

Vanessa was the first to notice her friend's approach and frowned at her. Vicky looked good in the tight, black dress and heels, but the strap of the bag she carried ruined the line. "What's that?" Vanessa pointed to the bag.

Vicky shrugged. She had tried to leave the annoying satchel at home, but it had weighed too heavily on her mind, so she went back to get it. Darien had told her to keep it with her at all times, and she didn't want to risk his needing something and her not having it.

Vicky looked at her tall friend and noticed Vanessa's long, red hair had been curled and styled to frame her beautiful face. "Work," she explained. "I'm on call, so I brought this with me in case I'm needed."

Vanessa rolled her eyes as Vicky unslung the bag and dropped it on the floor next to the booth. She took a seat with the other three girls, and they chatted about

53

their weeks as the waiter brought them drinks.

"I thought you were on call." Maggie giggled as Vicky took a long pull from her fruity drink.

Vicky smiled over her glass at the petite brunette. "Just because I'm *on* call doesn't mean he *will* call." Vicky took another sip as the rest of the girls joined Maggie laughing. "Anyway, I didn't drive, so if something comes up, I'll just have to take a cab."

The rest of the girls agreed this was a sensible idea.

"So what is this new job of yours?" Beth asked, from the other side of the table.

Vicky shrugged at the dark-haired girl. Looking over her three friends, she thought about the answer. "I'm a personal assistant," Vicky wasn't sure if she should fill them in on whom she was assisting.

"Ohh... a *personal* assistant," Maggie repeated, giggling even harder.

Vicky elbowed her. "Not like that!" She fumed at her friends teasing. "I keep my boss's life in order. You know: appointments, finances, running errands, that kind of thing. That's what is in the bag."

Her friends were still giggling as she shook her head.

"So what's your boss like?" Vanessa asked.

"He's just your normal businessman. He has enough meetings to run a racehorse ragged, but I guess that's to be expected in the corporate world." Vicky shrugged. "Otherwise, he's nice. A little absentminded at times. And he can be somewhat eccentric, but he treats me well, so I can't complain."

The girls nodded their approval.

"Is he cute?" Beth asked.

Vicky blushed as Darien's image came to mind. The giggles commenced around the table again. "I have to admit, he is handsome."

The girls perked up, so they wouldn't miss any of the details.

"Tall, with rich, brown hair and emerald-green eyes."

"Tall, dark, and handsome," Vanessa teased. "No wonder you don't mind being on call."

Vicky scoffed at her friend. "He's my boss!" She defended herself, making the other girls laughed again. "Now, if you're done teasing me about my gainful employment, do you want to go dance?"

Her friends poked at her in fun for a moment more before agreeing.

It didn't take them long to get lost on the dance floor. Vanessa was the first to pick up a guy, but the fact that she was built like a supermodel made it easy for her to get just about any guy she wanted.

Vicky had just started dancing with the friend of the guy Maggie was clinging to, when a familiar tune cut through the din of the club and grabbed Vicky's attention. She quickly excused herself from her dance partner and ran to the messenger bag to retrieve the phone. The guy followed her from the dance floor.

"Hello?" Vicky answered breathlessly, plugging up her other ear so she could hear what her boss was saying. She was surprised she had even heard the gentle tones of the phone over the heavy beat of the dance music.

"Sorry to disturb your night, Miss Westernly, but I need something from the satchel. Do you have it with you?"

Vicky could barely hear Darien's voice over the noise. She waved the guy she had been dancing with back with a mouthed response of "*my boss*," and disappeared into the bathroom.

"Sorry, Mr. Ritter, I couldn't hear you. Could you please say that again?" she asked as soon as the walls of the restroom held out most of the thumping music.

"I asked if you had your bag," he repeated.

"Yes, I've got it with me."

"Good. Where are you?"

"Alchemy, on the west side of town."

"That's not far. I'll see you out front in about ten minutes." Darien hung up before Vicky could respond to his request.

She pulled the phone away from her ear and looked at it. What was someone like him doing on this side of town?

When she stepped out of the bathroom, she found that her friends and the guys they had picked up were standing around the table waiting for her return. Vanessa had seen her bolt from the dance floor and had followed.

"My boss needs something from the bag." Vicky smiled at her friends as she gathered the satchel from the floor. She had kept a close eye on it all night, but no one had bothered it at all. "He is going to meet me out front in ten minutes."

Vicky's three friends all perked up when they heard that her mysterious boss was coming to the club. The prospect of meeting Vicky's tall, dark, and handsome employer overshadowed the men clinging to them. The girls paid out their tabs and promised the guys they'd be back after they had made sure their friend's boss was treating her right.

Vicky rocked on her heels as she waited for Darien to show up. The excitement from her three friends was tangible as they chattered about the possibilities.

"So, what's he like?" Vanessa prodded as they waited for the man to show up.

"I told you, he's just your average businessman." Vicky sighed.

"Ohh, I bet he's rich." Beth giggled. "He has to be well-off to have a personal secretary ready to do his every bidding."

Maggie agreed, making Vicky shoot them a frosty glare.

She rolled her eyes at her friends. "Of course he's rich. He runs the company."

Her friends giggled again. Vicky could tell they'd been drinking a little too much.

"I bet he's a hot, foreign guy," Maggie piped in. "Does he have an accent?"

"I would love a rich, hot guy with a foreign accent!" Beth moaned. "I *so* want him to be English, or even Scottish. I love listening to British guys talk!"

Vicky shook her head as their ideas got wilder and wilder. "Sorry to burst your bubble, but he doesn't have a cool accent."

"Oh, I know!" Vanessa added her idea to the pot. "Wouldn't it be great if he came from some mega-rich family, like a lost prince or a lord or something?"

"Yeah, a vampire lord out to drink your blood!" Beth added as her imagination worked overtime in her slightly drunken state. The others laughed at this outrageous idea.

Vicky sighed. "No, Beth, he's not a vampire. We work during the day. What kind of fiction do you read, anyway?"

The others picked up this train of thought and ran with it. By the time Darien finally showed up, the girls had reinvented Vicky's boss as a master vampire. Vicky had been given the role of the fair maiden who was seduced into being his courtesan and food.

When Vicky spotted the familiar Aston Martin pulling up to the curb, she shushed them, but the women didn't need any encouragement to be quiet. All three stood with their mouths open in awe at the little, black sports car. They were even more taken aback when Darien stepped from the car in a black dress shirt and slacks. He looked over at his assistant standing on the sidewalk in front of the club.

"He can bite me any day of the week," Vanessa whispered, just loud enough for the girls to hear. She was rewarded with a string of giggles from her friends and a stern look from Vicky.

"He doesn't have fangs. Now cut it out!" she hissed at her friends, trying to get them to be more serious. This was her boss they were talking about.

Darien smiled as he ran his tongue over the tip of one of his canines. If she only knew how pointy those teeth could get when he wanted them to. He'd heard everything the girls had said from the moment he had stepped out of the car. His hearing was exceptionally good.

"Good evening, Mr. Ritter." Vicky addressed him as professionally as possible, under the circumstances. She heard more giggles from her teasing friends and swore she was going to beat them as soon as her boss left.

"Good evening, Miss Westernly." Darien tried not to smile at her annoyance. "I'm sorry that I pulled you away from your fun, but I need something from inside that bag." He pointed to the black messenger bag.

"It's no problem." She pulled it off and handed it over

to her boss.

Darien took it to the back of his car, and Vicky grimaced when he plopped it down, unceremoniously, on the expensive car.

Maggie leaned forward and whispered into Vicky's ear. "That's not Darien Ritter?"

Vicky nodded her head, confirming the theory.

Maggie whistled her amazement. "How the hell did you get that job?" This was one of the most powerful men in Brenton, and Vicky was nobody.

"Temp agency," Vicky admitted.

Maggie nearly passed out. No one scored a job like this from a temp agency.

Darien muttered to himself as he dug into the bag, looking for something.

"Miss Westernly…"

His call drew Vicky's attention away from her awed friends.

"Can you come hold this for me?" He held out the leather books from inside the bag without looking up.

Vicky quickly stepped up to relieve him of the items.

"Thank you. They kept trying to slip off the back of the car."

She looked at the sloped back window and the short lip of the trunk and smiled. The back of an Aston Martin was definitely not a good place to empty out a bag.

Vicky was confused by her boss's actions. Darien had emptied most of the items out of the satchel, but he was still rummaging around, looking for something. She startled when he let out a sudden "Aha!" upon finding what he wanted deep in the folds. Looking on in surprise, she watched as he pulled out a rather worn, leather pouch she had never seen before.

Darien opened the pouch and dumped out a handful of colorful rocks. He picked out two large, green ones before sliding the rest back in. Tossing the small bag back into the satchel, he pocketed the stones before holding his hand out for Vicky to return the books she was holding. She gave them over, and he stuck them back into the bag and flipped the top over. Darien turned to face his assistant and handed the bag back to her. She eyed it warily before taking it and pulling the strap over her shoulder.

"It's dangerous out at night," Darien looked over the four women standing on the sidewalk. Turning his attention back to Vicky, he asked, "How are you getting home?"

Vicky opened her mouth to answer him.

"She's going to walk," Vanessa cut her off.

A tiny spark of annoyance lit his face as he pinned Vicky to the sidewalk with slightly narrowed eyes.

Turning her head, she yelled at her friend. "Not in these heels!" She looked back to her boss. "I was going to call a cab when we're done."

Darien nodded his approval. A cab would be better than walking or driving. He could smell the alcohol on her.

"But, we're already done here," Beth lied.

Vicky stared at her with wide eyes as Maggie and Vanessa both snickered.

"Yeah, I'm going to take these two home now," Vanessa informed him. "So, Vicky'll have to wait here for her cab by herself."

A devious grin curled the edges of Darien's lips. It was easy to see that these women were trying their best to get him to take Vicky home. He had a good idea what they were hoping would happen, but he decided giving her a lift would be better than leaving his assistant in the care of her drunken friends.

Walking over to his passenger door, Darien popped it open. "Get in." He spoke with a commanding tone that wouldn't allow Vicky to argue with him.

Looking from the open car door to her smiling friends, Vicky huffed before stomping over to the car. As Darien shut the door, she glared at the three girls waving from the sidewalk. She shook her finger at them, angrily letting them know she would get them for this later.

The girls laughed at her plight and turned to go back into the bar where their guys were waiting for them.

Vicky hung her head and shook it in exasperation as Darien slipped into the driver's seat. "I'm sorry about this, Mr. Ritter," she sighed. "I really don't know what's gotten into my friends tonight." She looked over at Darien's profile. "It's no problem for me to get a cab."

Just as she reached for the door handle, he clicked the electronic lock, cutting off any more argument from his passenger.

She shivered as he held her with a penetrating gaze. It was amazing how his eyes shimmered in the light from the car's console.

"Safety is important, especially late at night." Darien turned back to the road and eased the car away from the curb. "I really don't mind making sure you get home."

She folded her hands in her lap. "Thank you, but I don't want to keep you from what you were doing."

"Don't worry about it," he replied. "That old codger has been waiting for this prize a long time. It won't kill him to wait a little bit longer." Something else passed

61

across Darien's face as he spoke, "But *I* will, if I find out he was cheating."

She shuddered at the cold note in her boss's voice, and they rode for the rest of the trip in silence.

Darien pulled up in front of Vicky's apartment and turned to look at her. Relaxed against the seat, Vicky had nodded off during the trip home. Her head tilted over so her face was turned away from him, leaving the long line of her neck exposed. Darien felt the sharp points of his fangs against his lip as he thought about how tempting the soft skin over her pulse point was. He couldn't help thinking about how defenseless she was in that position. After considering it for a moment, he shook the thought away. It would be a bad idea to mix work with pleasure. He'd gone through a lot of trouble trying to find someone so well suited to his needs. It wasn't worth the risk of having to go through that hell again just for a little blood.

"We're here." Darien touched his assistant's shoulder to wake her up.

Vicky shook her head to clear her mind of the sleep that had overtaken it. She yawned into the back of her hand, breathing deeply as she stretched the sleep from her. Embarrassed, she realized she had fallen asleep. ."I'm so sorry, Mr. Ritter. Thank you for taking me home."

He smiled warmly at her. "You're quite welcome, Miss Westerly. Now, go get some rest."

Unable to get her eyes to focus properly on her boss's face, Vicky blinked several times before thanking him again and getting out of the car.

Darien waited around until she was safely inside before heading back to the game of chance he'd left to retrieve the two uncut emeralds from the depths of Vicky's bag.

Vicky dropped the mysterious bag on the couch as she headed to the bathroom to wash her face. Once clean, she changed out of her dress and crawled into her covers.

Studying the patterns on the kimono, she tried to sort out what had caused her to do a double take on the face of the handsome man that dropped her off. Vicky was sure it was just her sleep-addled mind and the stupid shenanigans of her friends that caused her to see things that weren't real. There was no way she had seen fangs poking out of the corners of her boss's mouth. Vicky closed her eyes and let herself slip back into dreams filled with thick, foreign accents, vampires, and brilliant, green eyes.

6

THE KEYS ON VICKY'S COMPUTER CLICKED AS SHE ENTERED THE data from the files piled on her desk. She had finally emptied out both of the boxes that Darien had left for her to organize. Between keeping her boss on time and running his random errands, it had taken her the better part of the week just to get the papers in something that resembled order. Now that they were sorted out, all she had to do was input the information into the spreadsheet she'd created. Once finished, she would have a clear and precise account of all the finances of the small company Darien was interested in picking up. It should only take another week of constant work for her to finish the job.

Her attention was pulled away from the figures when the door to the outer office swung open, and a large man walked in. Dressed in dark jeans and a red T-shirt under a black leather biker's jacket, the man stood a full head taller than Vicky did. His hair was dark brown and would have looked rather nice if he had combed it properly. As it was, he looked as if he had just run his fingers through his hair roughly. The stranger's heavy

65

boots carried him with intent towards Darien's office.

Vicky stood to greet the man before he could interrupt her boss's conference call. "Good afternoon, sir," she began. "Is there something I can do for you?"

The man ignored her and continued towards her boss's door.

Vicky quickly put herself between him and the door.

He stared at her, surprised. "I'm here to see Darien. Move," he growled.

She took a step back but didn't shift out of his way. "Mr. Ritter is busy at the moment," she informed the man glaring at her. "If you would like to make an appointment, I'd be happy to help you."

He growled at her again and took another step towards the inner office. "I'll see him now."

Vicky took another step back, so she was almost against the door. She raised her hands and placed them on the man's chest to stop his forward momentum. "I told you, he's busy now. Please don't make me have to call security."

Before she knew what was happening, the man grabbed her by the throat, lifted her up to his eye level, and pressed her into the wooden door. "I will see him *now*," he snarled into her face.

Vicky clawed at his hand as she gasped for air. She kicked at him, trying to get free. Dark spots filled her vision as pain radiated from where he was crushing the life from her. She tried to scream for help, but nothing would come out past the hurt being caused her. The last thought that passed through her mind before darkness engulfed her was that the stack of paperwork next to her desk would never get entered into the spreadsheets.

◆◆◇◆●◆◇◆◆

Darien opened his office door and caught the unconscious form of his assistant as she fell from his unannounced visitor's hand. He quickly gathered the un-breathing woman into his arms and transported her to his leather couch, knowing he would need to do something fast to save her life.

"Damn it, Rupert!" Darien cursed. "Why the hell did you go and do that?" He checked Vicky's pulse and found it thready.

"She's human?" Rupert said, slightly shocked, as he stepped into the room and shut the door. "With the way she was acting, I didn't realize she was. You can fix it, right?"

"Yes, but I'd rather not have to," he growled at his visitor before turning his mind to the girl who desperately needed his help.

Darien's unwelcome guest watched him work.

Rupert had done a fine job of crushing her trachea. Darien knelt next to Vicky and placed his right hand over the damaged area. Using his left hand, he pinched off her nose and tilted her head back slightly, so he could press his mouth firmly over hers. He blew gently into her mouth, trying to push some air into her lungs. As he did so, Darien released a tendril of power into the damaged area and forced the crushed windpipe back to its original shape. Tasting the blood bubbling up from her injury, he suppressed the shiver of excitement that always came with the taking of blood from a living being.

Once she could breathe again, Darien pulled away from her mouth, pushed back his vampiric nature, and centered himself so that he could complete the healing she still needed.

Now calmer, he drew another deep breath and

sealed his lips to hers once more. The rich taste of her fresh blood was hard to ignore, but he forced back the cravings and concentrated on rebuilding the injured tissue.

When the majority of the work was done, Darien pulled back from the life-giving kiss and sat back on the carpet to collect himself. He pushed up from the floor and turned his attention to the man watching from the other side of the room.

"What do you want, wolf?" Darien snarled with fangs in full view.

Rupert's eyes widened at the response from the normally calm vampire. He had seen Darien heal many times, but he had never seen this reaction before.

"Are you okay?" Rupert asked.

"Not really. Crushed throats lead to blood in the mouth. Very bad for one's control." Darien walked farther away from the source of his issues, yanked opened the window, and stuck his head out. He could still smell the fresh blood from his assistant.

"Sorry about that. I've just had a lot on my mind recently." Rupert rubbed the back of his neck and looked a little remorseful. He glanced back to the young woman resting on the couch. "I'd forgotten how fragile humans can be." He turned his attention back to Darien leaning out the window, drawing in the clean air. "I didn't think you all needed to breathe," the werewolf commented.

"We don't breathe when we sleep, bloody madra," he scolded him.

Rupert could see that Darien was regaining control. When the vampire turned around, his fangs were gone.

Darien leaned against the open windowsill with his arms crossed over his chest. "Now, what do you mean by coming here during business hours and accosting my employees?"

Rupert turned serious. "Have you heard about the recent murders?"

"The ones the reporters have dubbed the 'Southside Slaughters'?" Darien asked.

Rupert nodded.

"I've been following them in the papers. What about them?"

"There was another fire last night."

Darien shrugged at this information. "So?"

"The shredded victims were all my wolves," Rupert said grimly. He was the local pack alpha, and, although he was a rough man, he cared dearly for all the people in his pack.

Darien uncrossed his arms and stared at Rupert in shock. He had assumed that the torn up bodies had something to do with a rampant werewolf. Such things normally were, but for something to have torn up werewolves without being seen or heard by anyone was insane. "If these murders weren't caused by your kind, what did it?"

Rupert shrugged. "I was hoping you could help us find out," the alpha wolf explained. "There've been other strange happenings in the south side before the fires started, and we had been trying to track down the cause of the trouble. So far, we've been unsuccessful. I was hoping the Vampire Council would be able to help."

Darien looked at him, astonished. It had been a long time since the werewolves and vampires had gotten together to deal with anything. The last time had ended badly, and the two groups usually avoided each other like the plague. "You, of all people, should know there are difficulties between the vampires and the wolves," Darien pointed out.

Rupert nodded. "That's why I'm coming to you. You're the only one in town on neutral ground with both groups. Please, Master Darien," Rupert begged, "we can't handle this by ourselves."

Darien sighed deeply and pinched the bridge of his nose, trying to ward off the headache that he knew this would cause. How could he refuse a begging pack alpha? "All right," he relented, "but you owe me twice for this. Once for dealing with the Vampire Council and once for injuring my people. And, I expect you and yours to be nice to Miss Westernly in the future. She works too hard to be treated with such disrespect."

"You have my word." Rupert bowed deeply, accepting the demand of two boons. He would have given much more to ensure the safety of his pack. "Now, if you'll excuse me, I'd like to go visit my sister before leaving."

Darien waved him off with a growled warning not to disturb anyone else on his way out.

Rupert agreed, chuckling as he exited the office.

Darien looked over at the sleeping form of his assistant. He was going to have to get something to quiet his hunger before he really did sink his fangs into that undefended neck of hers.

Vicky tried to breathe deeply as she woke, but coughed when the air caught in a sore place in her throat. She let out a pained noise as she raised her hand to her neck and touched it gently. Her eyes opened to reveal an unfamiliar ceiling. Rolling her head over to look at the room around her, she was shocked to find she was lying down on the couch in Darien's office. Someone had placed a woven blanket across her to keep her warm.

Pulling herself into a sitting position, Vicky puzzled over how she got into this predicament. She could just remember the violent man lifting her against the door, but everything after that was missing. Vicky could see her boss working on some project at his desk. When she tried to stand up, her head spun violently, and she sat back down.

"Careful there." Darien got up from his work and sat on the edge of the couch next to where Vicky was hunched over. He pulled her up, so he could look in her eyes to make sure she would be okay. "You've had a nasty shock."

She moved limply under his gentle hands. "Is he gone?" Vicky croaked hoarsely. She swallowed, trying to soothe her sore throat.

Concern crossed Darien's face at how crackly her voice was. He was worried he had missed something important when he reconstructed her windpipe. "He's left and won't bother you again," Darien reassured her. "Let me have a look at your throat."

Vicky nodded lightly and tilted her head back, exposing the injury.

Placing his right hand behind her head to support her, he wrapped his left across the bruised skin of her neck, and pushed a bare hint of power into the damaged area, searching for the problem. Finding a split in the cartilage around her vocal cords, he snapped it back into place where it belonged. He could have healed her completely, but that would lead to some very hard questions that he didn't want to answer.

Vicky was in too much pain to disagree with her boss's invasion of her personal space. His hands felt good on the soreness of her neck. They were unusually warm, and the heat penetrated deep into her throat, soothing the hurt. She closed her eyes and relaxed as she let him feel her throat. A quick, sharp pain brought a cry from her lips, and she nearly passed out from the intensity of it. The only things that had kept her from collapsing to the cushions were the hands on her neck. Vicky panted as black spots danced behind her eyes. She felt Darien shift her so that she was lying down on the couch again.

"Rest here for a little longer," he said softly.

Vicky nodded without opening her eyes. She didn't feel as if she could get up at the moment, anyway.

He fluffed the blanket back over her and went to find her something to drink. Even though he had sped the healing process along, Vicky would need rest to allow the tissue to knit properly.

⋘⬤⋙

Vicky woke up to the more familiar ceiling of Darien's office. Her throat felt better, so she sat up slowly and looked around the dimly lit room.

Darien was using the light on the corner of his desk to fend off the growing darkness as he read through the thick stack of paperwork in his hands. He folded the papers back into a file and placed it lightly on his desk before coming to check on her. Vicky watched him approach.

"How are you feeling?" he asked.

Vicky cleared her throat lightly and smiled weakly. "Better," she whispered. The crackle was gone from her voice, but it was still tender to talk.

Darien nodded his approval and held out his hand so Vicky could use it to stand. "It's getting late. Let me take you home. You should be fine by morning," he reassured her.

"I'm sorry," Vicky whispered as she took hold of his hand and rose from the couch. She felt bad that she had slept for most of the day.

"Don't be." He patted her on the shoulder as they headed towards the door. "It's not your fault. You did a good job today."

Vicky looked at him skeptically and shook her head as she headed to her desk. Saving her work, she cleared away her project before picking up her bag, so Darien could take her home.

Holding the door for her, he let her lead the way.

Vicky was still unsure how to feel about the events of the day as she settled into the passenger seat of the familiar Aston Martin. She closed her eyes and thought about the man who had strangled her and the last thought that passed through her mind as she black out. A joyless laugh slipped from her.

"What's funny?" Darien asked, trying to coax Vicky's thoughts from her.

"Ironic more than funny."

He cocked an eyebrow, and Vicky continued.

"I was sure I was going to die when that guy had me pressed against the door, but it didn't happen." The day had been too surreal to scare her at the moment.

Darien was surprised at how well she was taking the near-death experience. Of course, he wasn't about to tell her how close she had actually come to dying. "What didn't happen?" he prodded.

She shrugged. "That whole 'life flashing before your eyes' thing. It didn't happen. No thoughts of my family or friends. Nothing about my past. The only thought that hit me was of the pile of folders sitting next to my desk, and how I wouldn't get the chance to enter them into the spreadsheets."

"Well, you don't need to worry about it now." Darien shot her a smile as he pulled out into the evening traffic. "You're fine, and you'll get the chance to get back to those files tomorrow."

Vicky let out a heavy sigh that made Darien chuckle. Turning her attention away from her boss, she stared out the window. The world slipped past, unseen, as her fingers found their way to the tender area of her neck. The sound of the cartilage in her throat giving way under the pressure of the man's hand had terrified her. She had been sure she was going to die, but here she sat with only a sore throat. How she had managed to escape her doom was beyond her, but she was sure it had something to do with the man driving her home. Unfortunately, she couldn't think of a good way to ask him. Nothing short of extensive surgery could fix a crushed trachea, and that obviously wasn't the case here. Maybe the terror and pain had made her think there was more injury than there really was. Vicky nodded her head as she settled on this explanation of the day's events. She had just passed out from lack of oxygen, and her mind had exaggerated the experience into something more serious than it was.

"Make sure you get something to eat before going to bed."

Vicky was pulled from her thoughts by Darien's words. She blinked for a moment until she realized they were sitting in front of her apartment building. "I will," she promised as she clambered out of the car. Turning around, she bent over, so she could look at the man who had taken such good care of her. "Thank you."

Darien smiled warmly at her. "You're quite welcome,

Miss Westernly. I'll see you tomorrow."

Vicky closed the door and found her way into her apartment before Darien pulled back out onto the street. Dropping her bag in its customary spot on the couch, she kicked off her shoes and headed into the kitchen to drop a package of ramen noodles in a pot. If she overcooked them a little, they would be soft enough to get down without hurting her already-tender throat.

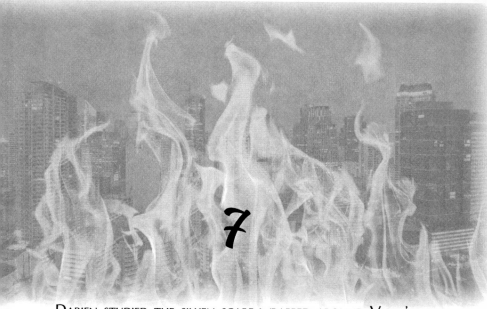

Darien studied the silken scarf wrapped around Vicky's neck. It was soft and flowing, and it accented her outfit quite nicely, but that wasn't the reason his assistant was wearing it. The scarf didn't quite cover all the bruising, but it was just the right color to make one question if the purpling seen around the edges was on the skin or part of the scarf.

"Good morning, Miss Westernly. How are you feeling today?"

Vicky raised a hand unconsciously to her throat before answering. "Much better. Thank you, Mr. Ritter." Dropping her hand, she fished into the plastic bag she was carrying. "I brought you something for taking care of me yesterday."

Darien cocked a curious eyebrow as Vicky pulled out a small, wooden crate and sat it gently on his desk. He laughed at the box of clementines. "You really didn't have to do that." Darien looked up at her with a warm expression.

"I know, but I wanted to." Vicky looked down shyly at the corner of the desk as she spoke. When he didn't respond, she glanced up find him staring at her. The intensity she found there made her cheeks warm.

"Thank you."

Vicky nodded in response. Darien's voice had taken on a more tangible quality than normal. Her blush deepened as his voice caressed her insides. Slipping back into professional mode, she said, "If there's nothing else at the moment, I'm going to run down to the café and get some coffee before hitting that paperwork. Would you like something?"

A grin curled one side of Darien's mouth. "No, but thank you."

Vicky nodded again and disappeared through the door.

Shaking his head, Darien considered the girl. It had been a long time since anyone surprised him as much as she did. He marveled at the graceful way she kept up with his hectic life while dealing with the more unpredictable bit of his nature.

Darien hadn't been sure what Vicky's mental state would be when she came in this morning. He had been prepared to deal with an emotional wreck, but she didn't seem shaken by the werewolf's attack at all. It would probably be a good idea to watch her for the next few days to make sure she wasn't in some state of shock. Nothing like that had happened in the three years Marianna had worked for him, but he was sure Vicky's predecessor would have quit over being nearly killed.

Pulling the wooden box towards him, Darien tugged the plastic mesh off, freeing the little oranges. He picked one up and rubbed his thumb across its skin as he pondered his new assistant. How much of his world could she handle before she ran away screaming? Pushing the thought away, Darien vowed he would do his best not to let it near her again. Vicky was much too innocent to deal with the world of the night.

"What's wrong?"

Sue's question pulled Vicky from her thoughts. She had zoned out while waiting for the young woman to finish making her drink.

Sue set the hot coffee on the counter and smiled encouragingly at her customer.

Vicky pursed her lips as she debated telling the barista about her issues. She didn't dare tell her normal friends about her recent attack. Vanessa would have her suing someone. Finally, she asked, "Have you ever been truly terrified for your life?"

Sue's eyes slipped to the scarf, and she smiled understandingly. "Yes," she admitted.

A puzzled look crossed Vicky's face as she thought about this answer for a second. "How do you cope with it?" She raised her hand to the scarf to make sure it hadn't slipped.

Sue gave her a worried look. "Did something happen with Mr. Ritter?"

Vicky was startled by the question. "No, not with Mr. Ritter." She shook her head. "There was an… incident with someone who came to visit him yesterday."

Sue's eyes widened a little as Vicky spoke.

"I've been reliving the experience in my mind all night, and it really has me freaked out. Sure, you hear about people getting hurt every day in the news, but you never imagine it could happen to you. I was almost afraid to get out of bed this morning."

"I can understand how that could shake your world

a bit." Sue sighed, pulling a large, chocolate chip cookie from the case and placing it on the counter with Vicky's coffee. "There are two things you can do. Either you can let them win and go through life in a constant state of fear, or you can use it to become stronger. Yes, there are violent people out there, but there are also a lot of good people. If you shut yourself up to avoid one, you miss out on the opportunity to meet the other."

Vicky smiled weakly as she mulled over Sue's words. "Thank you." She picked up the coffee and cookie. "You've given me a lot to think about."

"Anything I can do to help." Sue waved Vicky off and turned back to tend to her coffee machines.

As Vicky headed back to her office, she took a bite from the cookie and found that it was still slightly warm. She smiled, licking the sweetness from her lips. Nothing sets the world right like slightly melted chocolate from a fresh-baked cookie.

8

"WE'LL NEED TO LEAVE IN ABOUT TEN MINUTES."

Darien looked up from his desk to acknowledge the words of his assistant. He was glad to see her throat had finally healed enough for her to stop wearing those damn scarves. She had several that she coordinated with her outfits, but it was clear that they bothered her. A week and a half of her incessantly fidgeting with the scraps of material was almost more than Darien could stand.

He slipped the folder of notes into his desk drawer and stood up to look at his reflection in the rain-spattered glass. Today's weather was not the best for his weekly visit with Mr. Rodgers, but he needed to pick up the progress reports from his car-loving associate. He had already pushed their normal, Thursday-morning meeting to Friday afternoon. "Is everything ready?" Darien turned to look at Vicky waiting for him by the door.

"I've already called down to Charlie to make sure the car is ready," she answered, "and Gracie Ann from Cacophony called to cancel her appointment this afternoon, so we don't have to rush. Seems the roof of her building sprung a leak, and she has everyone moving the instruments around so they won't get wet."

Darien's brow creased as he worried about the little music store he had started backing. Ritter Enterprises had begun as a shipping corporation, but Darien loved to dabble in small businesses that were unable to get financial assistance by normal means. Even though her credit was abysmal, Gracie Ann had pleaded such a strong case that he just couldn't say no. Once it was established, he had been very pleased with the way she ran the shop. But something like this could really cause her problems.

"Has she called someone yet?" Darien asked.

"Already taken care of," Vicky informed him with a smile. "I called Rick's Roofing. He'll look at it tomorrow when the rain has stopped."

Darien snickered. Of course Vicky would ask another one of his small businesses to deal with Gracie Ann's problem. "Very nice. Now, let's go see what Charlie's picked for us today." Darien led the way out of the office.

Vicky paused long enough to grab up her messenger bag as she passed her desk.

He glanced at the stack of files next to Vicky's desk as he passed. It didn't look any smaller than it did on the day she had placed it there. "How is your project coming?" Darien asked, pushing the button to call the elevator.

"Pretty good, actually," she informed him. "It should only take about a day or two of steady work to enter the rest of the information." She gave a small sigh as they entered the elevator and Darien sent it to the underground basement. "I was hoping to have it finished by today, but it took me longer than I anticipated." Vicky's hand moved to her throat as she recalled the reason she was behind.

Over the days following the incident, Darien had watched as Vicky dealt with the feelings left from Rupert's heavy-handed treatment. At first, he had been worried. More than once, he caught her playing with her scarf while staring off into space. Evidently, she had come to some kind of terms with it. She seemed back to her normal self again.

Darien let Vicky lead the way to the guardhouse, where Charlie was waiting. She had learned that the old man was less of a guard and more of a caretaker to Darien's extensive car collection. Charlie did all the upkeep and maintenance needed to keep the machines purring the way they should.

"Whatcha' got for us today?" Vicky asked, bouncing as she waited for the old man to give up the keys to the car they were going to take. She wasn't really a car nut, but there was something about the classic ones that got her a little excited.

Charlie greeted her with a wide grin. "I've something special for you, today." He held up a key on a worn, leather fob. "A 1970 Ford Torino Fastback."

Vicky giggled with delight and reached for the key, but Darien was just a hair faster and closed his hand around the bit of metal before his assistant could.

"I want this one."

Vicky dropped her hand and grinned at her boss. She knew this was going to happen as soon as Charlie had said what today's transportation would be. Darien would often let her drive the cruising cars, but he usually wanted to drive the muscle cars himself.

"Bay 632." Charlie released the leather fob and pointed down into the garage. "It's raining, so be careful with her."

Darien stuck his finger through the key ring and twirled the key as he headed down the garage.

"Of course we will," Vicky reassured the man, hurrying to follow Darien before he left without her. She loved the days when they went to visit Mr. Rodgers. The car nut that ran the shipping hub on the north side of town almost always had positive news, and that put her boss in an especially good mood. Except for occasional bits of randomness, Darien was very professional, but Vicky suspected that hidden inside that polished exterior was an excitable and lighthearted person. These were the days the fun-loving guy poked his head out a little.

Sliding into the maroon bucket seats of the red muscle car, Vicky tucked her bag onto the floorboard by her feet. She watched a smile split her boss's face as he turned the key and the well-tuned V8 roared to life. The music that issued from the speakers was an older tune. Charlie always preset the radio to something just right for that car. The look on Darien's face when he drove one of these classics reminded Vicky of a kid set loose in a candy store. The joy radiating from him was infectious.

Vicky giggled a little as Darien pressed down on the gas and the car growled in delight at being let out of its little cage. She waved to the thoughtful caretaker as they passed on their way out into the rain-soaked world. Vicky settled in for the forty-minute ride to the north side of town.

Darien listened to Vicky humming along with the song on the radio as they pulled into the bay of the shipping company. The drive over had been more taxing then normal due to the heavy rain and stupid people unable to drive in it. There had been a rather large accident on the highway, which had slowed their progress down. Vicky had called ahead to let Mr. Rodgers know they were going to be late, but it had taken over two hours to get past the mangled cars blocking up the roadway.

Stepping out of the car, Darien stretched the fatigue from his limbs.

"I'm glad to see you made it all right."

He turned towards the short, stout, middle-aged man coming to greet him.

"That is fantastic." Mr. Rodgers looked over the sleek lines of the car.

"Thank you." Darien shook the man's outstretched hand before turning his attention to the car.

Vicky stepped out of the car to join the boys. She exchanged pleasantries with the head of the shipping hub before the men got lost in the details of the machine in front of them.

"Let me guess…" Mr. Rodgers almost bounced as Darien opened the flat, black hood to show off the heart of the car. "1970 Ford Torino Cobra Fastback! Ooh… you have the 429 SCJ V8 in it!"

Vicky smiled at the two overgrown kids. She caught a few words she recognized, like 'Holly' and 'Detroit Locker', but she had no idea how those things applied to a carburetor or rear differential. She left the two prattling on about the benefits of 'ram air induction' and 'shaker hoods' and went to gather the information that Darien had made the trip for.

"Good evening, Vicky," Mr. Rodgers' secretary

greeted her as she stepped into the main office. "How was the ride over?"

"Hey, Mary. It was horrible," Vicky confessed. "There was an accident that had traffic completely stopped for nearly an hour. What do you have for us today?" She pulled out a chair, so they could get things done. Vicky and Mary had gotten into the habit of holding the meeting their bosses were supposed to have, while the men chatted over whatever toy Darien had brought over to show off.

"Nothing much," Mary admitted as she slid the files over for Vicky to look at. "The numbers all look good this week."

Vicky flipped open the folders to check the stats.

"We did finally get a permanent driver to take the eastern run."

"That's good." Vicky nodded at the progress.

"You're telling me. I was getting tired of listening to Mr. Rodgers grumble about the temps we were being sent." Mary pushed her glasses up and rubbed the spot between her eyebrows. "Another week of that, and I was going to start driving the truck just to shut him up."

Vicky grinned at the idea of the petite brunette behind the wheel of an eighteen-wheeler. "I'm glad you didn't have to. I would miss our weekly chats."

"Not as much as they would," Mary nodded her head towards the men outside. "If we weren't here to take care of business, they wouldn't have time to talk about their cars."

Vicky agreed, and the two women went over the things that had happened during the week. Mr. Rodgers would tell Darien anything important during the time they chatted, but they would leave the fine details up to the girls. When Vicky and Mary finished, Vicky folded up the file and slipped it into her bag. "Want to walk to the break room with me? I need to get something to drink." Standing up, Vicky pulled the strap of her bag over her shoulder.

Mary agreed, and the two women chatted about their lives outside of work as they walked to the vending machines. Vicky picked up tea for herself and water for Darien, and they were on their way back to the shipping bay when music came from Vicky's bag. Mary's words failed at the eerie song.

Vicky fished the cell phone Darien had given her from her bag. "Hello?" Vicky answered, expecting to get Darien wondering where they were.

There was a long pause before an unfamiliar voice spoke. "May I please speak with Master Darien?" the thick, warm, male voice asked.

Vicky slipped into her professional voice. "Mr. Ritter is in a meeting at the moment. May I take a message and have him call you back?" She quickly pulled her notepad out, so she could jot down a message or number.

There was another long pause before the man answered her. "Tell him we'll be gathered at sunset, awaiting his arrival." The line clicked dead without giving Vicky a chance to ask anything.

Who was gathered? Where? She stared at the silent phone before folding it up and slipping it back into her bag. The caller ID didn't show a name or number, just 'Private'. She hoped Darien would understand the cryptic message.

"Everything okay?" Mary asked as they started back towards the shipping bay.

Vicky nodded. "Apparently, someone wants to see

Mr. Ritter tonight." She frowned a little. "The guy wasn't very clear."

Mary patted Vicky on the shoulder. "I get those for Mr. Rodgers from time to time," Mary opened the door to the shipping bay and held it for her guest. "He always seems to know what they're about."

Vicky stepped out and nodded. She didn't go into the fact that the call had come in on the strange phone Darien had given her. As far as she knew, her boss was the only person who knew that number.

The two women found their bosses still going on about the muscle car.

"And, it'll do a quarter mile in 13.99 seconds at 101." Darien's boasting earned him a long whistle from his friend.

"Pardon the intrusion," Vicky slipped into pause in their conversation. "I just got a call for you, Mr. Ritter. Do you have a meeting set up for this evening?"

Darien gave her a confused look. "Not that I'm aware of." He pondered who could have called his assistant. "Who was it?"

"I have no idea," Vicky shook her head. "He just said they'd be waiting for you after sunset."

A strange look crossed Darien's face, and he pulled his phone from his pocket to find that the battery was dead. "Pardon me, Mr. Rodgers. It seems I've forgotten something this evening." Darien shut the hood of the car.

"Then don't let me keep you." Turning to Mary, Mr. Rodgers asked, "Did Miss Westernly get everything she needed?"

Mary nodded.

Vicky said goodbye and got into the car. Whatever Darien had forgotten seemed pressing. Her boss bid his farewell and climbed into the car. It took no time for them to get back out into the rain and zooming down the highway.

"I'm sorry, Miss Westernly," Darien apologized very seriously. "I wasn't expecting this today. It's quite a drive to where I need to be tonight, and I don't have time to take you back to the office."

Vicky wasn't sure what was going on, but she had never seen him so tense.

"I'm going to head straight out there and let you drive back by yourself."

"That's fine with me, but how will you get back?"

"Don't worry about that. I just want to make sure you're safe."

Vicky gave him a confused look. Something about that statement bothered her.

"What did you get from Mary?" he asked to distract her from the questions floating just behind her eyes.

She shook her odd feeling away and pulled the business file from her bag to summarize it for him.

Darien didn't hear a word she said. He was too busy preparing to spend the evening with the Vampire Council.

9

"DAMN IT!" DARIEN CURSED AS HE HIT THE DEBRIS THAT THE CAR in front of him kicked up. Due to the heavy traffic, he had been unable to swerve out of the way, but he'd done his best to straddle the chunk of tire tread bouncing down the road.

Vicky covered her mouth to hide her smile. A string of rather colorful words issued from her boss as the garbage thumped along under the car. She had never heard such things slip past his lips before.

"Charlie's going to tan my hide if anything happens to the car."

"I thought these were your cars?"

"They may be my cars, but they're Charlie's babies." Darien chuckled at the love the old man lavished on the machines in his care.

Vicky's smile widened as she nodded. She could just imagine the hours Charlie spent rubbing wax onto the vast collection Darien kept squirreled away in that garage.

Darien took the exit ramp off the interstate and hit a county road that took them farther north. The storm was starting to wane, and the tail end of the day was just peeking through the thinning clouds.

Letting her mind wander, Vicky rode on in silence, watching the cornfields roll past. She was pulled from her thoughts by another string of indecent words from her normally proper boss. From where she sat, Vicky could see the little dials on the dashboard telling them that the engine temperature was much too high.

Darien continued to mutter as he pulled the car over to a wide spot in the road and got out to see what had gone wrong.

Vicky climbed out so she could help if he needed it.

Darien lifted the hood and looked down at the V8 steaming in the drizzle. He popped open the overflow bottle and looked in it before pulling a handkerchief from his pocket. Using the cloth to insulate his fingers, he twisted the hot radiator cap open to check the water level inside.

Vicky could remember her father doing this many times on the clunkers he drove, but the steam that came out was nowhere near as strong as it should have been.

Darien squatted down and placed his hand on the bumper of the car as he looked underneath. "We must have broken the radiator hose when we hit that junk." He sighed as he stood and looked up and down the road for an answer to their problems. There were no signs of life on the little road. Darien cursed his luck again and turned to ask Vicky for her phone, but she was gone. He found her digging in the glove box of the car.

"How far do we have to go?"

The question surprised Darien. "Another twenty miles or so," he answered, watching her pull the key from the ignition switch and climb back out of the car.

She dropped her suit jacket on the seat and rolled up her sleeves. Opening the trunk, she looked inside and made a disappointed noise before shutting the lid again. Only a spare tire.

Confused by her actions, Darien followed her around to the front of the car, where they both squatted down to look at the damaged hose. "What are you thinking?" he asked as he watched the wheels in Vicky's mind turning.

"I'm thinking that I'm going to need a new pair of stockings," she answered, and stood up.

To Darien's surprise, the woman turned from him and pulled up the hem of her skirt. She freed the top of her silk stocking from the garter holding it in place. Slipping out of her shoes, she pulled the first of the sheer tubes off.

Darien stood up and stared at her. He had no idea how taking off her stockings was going to help their situation.

When Vicky had them both in hand, she sat down on the wet ground in front of the car and wiggled underneath.

"What are you doing?" he asked, looking down through the engine compartment to see his assistant threading the delicate material around the damaged hose.

"I once watched my dad nurse a pickup truck with a damaged radiator hose fifty miles to town with only two gallons of water and a shop rag," Vicky explained as she twisted the first stocking into place and tied it as tight as she could. "He wrapped the cloth around the crack, so it held the hose together." She added the second stocking to the first. "I figured we could make it twenty miles if we could just get this tied off."

"With stockings?" Darien questioned her judgment.

"With *silk* stockings," she corrected. "Silk is a very strong material, especially when it's wet." Vicky checked her knots and pulled herself out from under the car.

"You wear silk, thigh-high stockings?" Darien asked, reaching down to help his assistant from the ground. This was another thing he hadn't expected from her.

Vicky blushed a little at his question. "One of the guys I dated in college got me started on them." The red on her cheeks deepened as she thought about the reasons her ex-boyfriend wanted her to wear them. "I found they were more comfortable than other options. And the silk ones are more durable then the nylon ones."

Vicky pulled away from Darien's hand and gathered her shoes to take back to the car. She pulled out her tea and the bottle of water Darien hadn't touched and brought them around to the front of the car.

"That's not going to be enough," Darien shook his head in mirth as Vicky emptied the bottle of water into the radiator.

"I know." She took one final swig of her drink before upending the liquid into the car. Vicky looked at the sky as the rain began picking back up, "You better get back in before you get soaked." She handed Darien the key and ushered him back into the car. "There's no reason for both of us to get wet, and you still have a meeting this evening."

Finding it hard to argue with the woman's logic, he let her put him back in the car and shut the door right before the rain cut loose. He watched Vicky collect the two bottles and make her way to the ditch, where a swelling stream of water was flowing past. Darien sighed helplessly as he waited for his assistant to finish, so they could get back underway.

It took several trips into the muddy ditch to get enough water to fill the radiator. Once full, Vicky signaled Darien to start the motor up and checked to make sure her makeshift patch was holding. Pleased with her work, she shut the hood. The dirt she had gotten on her back when she first laid down had been washed away while she worked, but there was still some on her legs. Pausing at a puddle, she cleaned the remaining traces of mud from her calves before opening the door. Since she was now soaked to the bone by the cold liquid falling in sheets from the sky, she stopped long enough to arrange her coat on the seat to protect the upholstery before sitting down gingerly.

Looking over at his drenched assistant, Darien turned the heater in the car up as far as it would go. He studied the woman who had just fixed his car. She huddled on the very edge of the seat with her arms wrapped tightly around herself, trying, unsuccessfully, not to drip on anything. Her hair had come loose and hung in rivulets about her shoulders, over her white shirt. The sheer material clung to her skin, and he could see what she wore underneath without even trying.

She tucked her bare feet under the dash, where the warm air could blow down on them.

"You could've worn your shoes," Darien sighed. It had killed him to watch her climb in and out of that ditch barefoot.

Vicky shook her head as she shivered. "High heels and mud don't mix." Her teeth chattered as she answered him.

Darien struggled out of his coat and flipped the warm material over Vicky's shoulders.

"Don't," she protested. "You'll need your jacket." She tried to stop the dry material from touching her.

Darien dropped it on her and made sure Vicky tucked it around herself. "Not as much as you do." He shifted the car into gear and pulled back onto the road.

Thanking him, she pulled the material tighter around herself.

Darien's mind turned over the new problem he now faced. There was no way he was going to let Vicky try to drive the damaged car back to the city tonight, and it would take Charlie at least three hours to get a wrecker out here to pick the car up. With Vicky soaked to the bone, she could catch a terrible cold during the six hours it would take to get back to the office. He could see no way around it; he was going to have to take her with him. It would be the first time he had ever called on the hospitality of the Council for someone other than himself.

"Given the circumstances, I'm going to ask my associates for help when we arrive."

Vicky looked up at Darien's softly spoken words.

"The people you're going to meet tonight can be a little unusual. If they make you uncomfortable, have them call me. I'll come as quickly as I can."

She nodded. "You don't think I'll be too much of a bother for them?" she asked, knowing the types of problems unexpected guests could cause. A strange smile crossed Darien's face.

"It's not them I'm worried about."

"We're here."

Darien's voice drew Vicky from her thoughts as they pulled into the courtyard of a grand mansion. It was two stories tall and looked like something that should have been sitting in the English countryside, not out in the middle of Nowhere, America. The driveway circled around a fountain that Vicky could just make out. Their pit stop had delayed them slightly, and full night was eating away at the fading twilight. Vicky slipped into her shoes and reached to pick up her messenger bag.

"You won't need that here," Darien placed his hand over hers before she could lift the bag from the floor.

Dropping it back, she stepped out of the car and wrapped herself tighter in Darien's coat in a vain attempt to hold off the cold wind trying to cut through her. She followed her boss up the steps of the large house. A tall man dressed in a tailcoat opened the large, wooden door for them.

The butler bowed as they passed. "Good evening, Master Darien. They are expecting you."

Vicky followed closely behind Darien as they walked into the grand foyer. She usually respected people's personal space, but there was something ominous about the extravagant hall that made her want to huddle into her boss's familiarity. Shaking this irrational fear away, she stepped back to stand on her own.

Noting her reaction to the new environment, Darien schooled the amused smile off his face.

A short woman in a long sundress appeared out of one of the side halls at a dead run. "Darien!" she squealed.

Vicky stepped back as the young woman threw herself at Vicky's boss.

He caught the girl in his arms, laughing.

The heavy atmosphere imposed by the grand house

was instantly shattered as she watched the professional man she knew transform into someone completely different.

He spun around with the girl in his arms, laughing, before placing her back on her feet. "You have gotten so big, Tiffany." Darien smiled.

Vicky was surprised to find that what she had taken for a short woman was, in fact, a very young teenager.

"If you'd come around more often, you'd see me growing," she teased, before turning her attention to the unannounced guest.

Darien waved for Vicky to step forward to be introduced. "This is Victoria Westernly. We had some problems on the way here. I ask that she be properly cared for tonight."

"Anything for you, Master Darien," the girl beamed.

"Miss Westernly, this is Tiffany," Darien introduced the girl. "She's the daughter of the housekeeper, Natalie."

Vicky shook the teen's hand.

"Tiffany, please make sure that everyone knows Miss Westernly is my guest this evening. She's an Innocent, and I don't want anything to happen to her."

Tiffany nodded. Taking Vicky by the hand, she pulled her away.

Vicky looked back to Darien. She wasn't sure what her boss had meant by that last statement, but she did not like it.

Seeing her reluctance to go, Darien waved to her. "Don't worry, Victoria. Tiffany will take care of you."

Thrown by the use of her first name, Vicky was pulled away from the foyer by the teen.

10

VICKY GATHERED UP HER MIND AND LISTENED TO THE STRING OF chatter from the excitable girl tugging on her arm.

"...He has been alone for such a long time that mother worries about him. Master Darien has never brought anyone here before. And the first person he does bring, he wants to keep to himself. I think it's great he's finally found someone he wants to keep."

Vicky wasn't sure she understood what the girl was going on about, but she needed to make sure Tiffany understood her relationship with Darien.

"Mr. Ritter and I are not dating," she informed the girl.

Tiffany looked up at her, smiling. "Of course not. I know how these things work."

Vicky was stunned by the girl's words. Surely, she hadn't just suggested that she and Darien were having an affair? This was something Vicky felt the need to set right. "I don't think you understand. I work for him." Embarrassment colored her cheeks as she tried to explain her position.

"You don't have to be embarrassed by that. Everyone

here receives something in return for it." Tiffany led Vicky through a door and into what looked to be the kitchen.

Vicky sputtered in shock. How could such a young girl talk about sex like that!

"Mom, Darien brought a guest!" the girl squealed in delight.

Vicky looked from the shocking girl to the woman standing over the stove. Both women had the same curly, brown hair and high cheekbones. It was very easy to see that they were related.

"Did he, now?" The woman wiped her hands on her apron and walked over to them. "I'm Natalie," she said, holding her hand out for Vicky to shake.

Vicky pulled her arm out from under Darien's jacket and shook the offered hand. "Victoria Westernly."

Natalie looked over the wet woman, shivering in her kitchen. "Let's get you cleaned up." She led the way back out into the hall. "What happened?"

"We broke a radiator hose on the way over, and I got caught in the rain trying to fix it."

Natalie held a door open for Vicky to enter. "Is Master Darien as wet as you are?"

"No. He got back in the car before the rain cut loose."

Natalie pursed her lips together. She didn't like that any man would make a woman fix the car while he stayed dry... master vampire or not.

"Let me introduce you to the rest of the gang." Natalie pointed to each person as she named them. "That's Brian and Jenny, Marsha, Roger, Terrance, Josephine, and Liz. I'm sure you'll run into everyone else during the rest of your stay." Addressing the group now facing her, Natalie said, "This is Victoria Westernly. She came here with Master Darien."

A murmur of surprise passed through the group at this introduction.

Natalie ignored their reaction and went on. "Can you see to her needs?"

"Of course, Nat, just leave her to us," the woman Natalie had pointed out as Josephine got up to take charge of the new arrival.

"Thanks, Josie." Natalie waved goodbye to Vicky. "They'll take good care of you."

Vicky was still reeling from everything that had happened since she had arrived, but she followed the new woman deeper into the room where the group of strangers was waiting.

"What happened?" a dark-haired man with delicate features asked.

Fishing in her mind, Vicky pulled out the name Terrance. "I got caught in the rain when the car broke down," she explained.

"That's horrible!" The raven-haired girl Natalie had called Liz answered.

"Do you need someone to look at it?" A handsome blond sat up from where he lounged on one of the many couches.

Vicky shook her head. "It has a blown radiator hose. I'm sure Mr. Ritter will call Charlie to come get it."

"You must be freezing." A tall, thin, black woman stood up, drawing Vick's attention. "What you need is a nice soak in the onsen."

Vicky heard agreement from all, and she found herself pulled into a protective hold as the woman spun her around to lead her back out of the room.

The entire group accompanied them down the

hallway and through a set of bamboo and paper doors. Vicky was surprised to find the doors concealed a large changing room. The seven people accompanying her spread out to different areas, pulled down baskets, and started stripping their clothing off.

Shocked, Vicky twirled around to face the wall and turned the deepest shade of red she could get.

"Is there something wrong, darling?" The tall, muscular man next to her asked as he folded his boxer shorts into the basket and slipped it back up onto the shelf.

Vicky squished her eyes shut as tightly as she could.

"I think she's shy," the voice of the little goth girl snickered from behind her.

"Don't tease her, Marsha." The voice of the delicate man reprimanded her. "She may not be used to such large groups. Master Darien has never brought us anyone before."

A collective agreement sounded around the room.

Vicky felt a reassuring pat from the naked man next to her.

"It's okay, darling. You're safe with us." She heard him turn to face the rest of the room. "Jenny, Josie, will you stay and make sure she's okay?"

The two girls agreed, and the man addressed the rest. "Everyone else get out to the bath so she can change."

"But Brian, I want to help too."

Vicky could hear the teasing note in the voice of the man that had offered to look at Darien's car.

"Get out of here, Roger," Brian growled.

Vicky calmed as the majority of the group left. Hearing two giggles, Vicky opened her eyes to see the tall, dark-skinned woman, who had to be Jenny, and the shorter blonde with long hair that was Josie.

"Is that better, sweetie?" Jenny came over and pulled an empty basket from the shelf, placing it on the floor in front of Vicky.

"Sorry," Vicky whispered. She pulled off Darien's jacket and folded it neatly into the basket. "I'm just not use to being around naked people."

The girls looked at each other, then back at Vicky.

"You're not a virgin, are you?"

Vicky blushed again at the question from Josie, trying to explain her embarrassment. "No, I just... am used to being around one person at a time."

The two women nodded their heads understandingly. Of course Darien would want an innocent girl for his companion. He never joined in the large bacchanals that would sometimes happen at the end of the functions. And he was always picky about his food, usually choosing someone with a bit more reserve.

"It's okay, sweetie," Jenny reassured her. "We're all good friends here. We'll look out for you."

Vicky nodded as she peeled off the layers of drenched cloth and folded them up. She looked down at Darien's jacket and pulled it out of the basket, so she could drop the wetter clothing in the bottom before draping the expensive suit coat over top.

Now naked, Vicky lifted the basket up and placed it on the shelf before turning to the other nude women in the room. She felt as if she should cover herself up, but there were no towels, and it would look funny if she tried to hide behind her hands while the other two were so casual about their nudity. She settled for wrapping her arms across her chest and rubbing the cold from them.

"Let's go get you warm," Josie held open the curtain

that separated the changing room from a prep area. "Have you ever been to an onsen before?" she asked.

"I don't even know what an onsen is," Vicky admitted.

Josie and Jenny grinned at each other.

"It's a large bath," Jenny informed her. "We'll get you set up." She hooked an arm around Vicky and led her to a row of low faucets and stools along the wall. Several bottles of soap sat along a ridge in the wall. Jenny deposited Vicky on one of the short stools in front of the faucets.

"It's customary to wash before getting into the pool," Josie informed her as she turned Vicky's water on to a nice, warm level and pulled down some soap for herself. Both Josie and Jenny wasted no time getting wet and soapy.

Testing her water, Vicky adjusted the temperature before scrubbing herself clean. The warm water felt good on her cold skin. Once all the soap was rinsed away, the three women got up from the washing area. Vicky followed her hosts through another door into an area containing a large pool.

She gasped as she looked over the room. Someone had done an amazing job making the steaming pool look like a large hot spring. The edges were all curvy and uneven, and the walls had been painstakingly painted to look like the side of some mountain. Vicky was so awed by the magnificent scenery that she didn't register the people sitting in the pool.

"Maybe she's not as shy as we thought."

The voice of the goth girl drew Vicky's attention to the group lounging in the water, and the red that had faded from her skin returned in full force. She faltered in her steps, but Josie and Jenny each hooked an arm and propelled her towards the warm water, where everyone was waiting for the new arrival.

"Be nice, Marsha." Brian snapped at the goth girl.

Marsha stuck her tongue out at the muscular man and dropped deeper into the water.

"Don't mind her, darling." He stood up and held out his hand for her.

Josie and Jenny both handed her off, so she had no choice but to take the man's hand and let him help her into the water. She was surprised to find that the large pool was hotter than the baths she took at home. There was a ledge along the edge, and the water level was just deep enough to cover her chest if she sat on the shelf.

Once the three girls were settled, Brian returned to his seat and leaned back against the wall to relax. Vicky was glad he was far enough away that he didn't crowd her.

"Be careful, sweetie," Jenny warned from where she rested in the pool. "The hot water can go to your head very quickly. If you feel faint, just let us know, and we'll get you out."

Vicky nodded. The hot water did wonders to drive out the chill that had settled into her bones.

They had only been in the water for a few minutes when Terrance popped the question everyone wanted to know. "What's he like?"

Vicky gave the delicate man a questioning look.

"Master Darien. What's he like?"

She could see that the entire group was hanging on the words she was about to say. "I really don't know how to answer that. I've only known Mr. Ritter for a few weeks now."

The group encouraged Vicky to tell them what she

did know.

"Um… he is very professional, and sometimes he can be very demanding, but he treats me well." She didn't think Darien would want her to tell them about his occasional randomness. Then again, given the bizarre behavior of this group, maybe it would be normal for them.

"Have you ever met any of Master Darien's others?" Liz asked from where she sat on the side of the pool.

Vicky wasn't exactly sure what she meant, but she assumed the woman was asking about the other temps that hadn't worked out. "No, they were all gone before I came along."

Worried sounds came from the group.

"Do you know how many he has gone through recently?" Jenny asked.

"I think there were nine in the two months between the time Marianna was put on bed rest and I was sent to him," Vicky answered. It had been one of the many topics that she had gossiped with Sue about.

The group looked at her with concerned eyes. They knew some masters could be hard on their servants, but to go through ten people in such a short period of time made them worry for Vicky's safety. The only master that was anywhere near that hard on his people was Michael, and his tastes changed fast enough to prevent the death of any one person.

"I always thought Master Darien was better than that," Liz said, shaking her head.

"Oh, darling." Brian shifted, so he could pull Vicky into a hug. "If there's anything we can do to help, please let us know."

Vicky froze as his arms came down around her. She

didn't understand the sudden outpouring of care and tried to move out of his arms, only to find Roger had come over to sit on her other side. Vicky's skin flushed as the blond man joined the muscular man holding her.

"We'll be here for you." Roger wrapped his arms around her, too. She squirmed as the two naked men held on to her. "Just let us know. Even if Master Darien isn't part of the Council, there has to be something they can do about it."

Vicky didn't understand why they were so upset. "Really, it's all right," she replied, trying to convince them she wasn't in trouble. "I enjoy what I do, and it pays well."

The two men pulled back a little, and Vicky took the opportunity to move away from the wall and float into deeper water. "I wouldn't want to go back to what I was doing before this." She shuddered at the thought of selling plasma to pay her rent again.

"That is not acceptable." Josie floated over to Vicky. "He should know better. We'll talk with our Masters about this. None of them could stand up to Master Darien alone, but all of them together should be able to stop him." Josie knew that the Council wouldn't stand for any vampire risking exposing the rest. If Darien were killing that many people, they would put a stop to it. The days when vampires left piles of dead bodies in their wakes were long over.

"I appreciate the help, but really, I'm fine." Vicky stood up quickly in the water to back away from the woman and clutched at the light feeling in her head. The random line of questioning had confused her enough that she hadn't realized she was overheating.

Josie reached for Vicky as she passed out and fell into the water. She quickly flipped Vicky over and pulled her to the edge of the pool to have Brian and Roger lift her from the water. Marsha ran for a towel to fan the fainted woman with. The others gathered around to make sure Vicky would be okay.

"For someone living with a Master that's so hard on his food, she looks to be very healthy," Terrance pointed out as they examined Vicky's body. "She doesn't have any fang marks." He turned her head, so he could inspect her neck closely.

"Maybe he bites her in less obvious places," Marsha suggested, and the group proceeded to check the rest of Vicky's skin for any signs of wounds. They even checked the femoral artery on her inner thigh, but they didn't find a single tooth mark.

"We can always ask her tomorrow, when she's feeling better," Jenny suggested.

They all agreed.

"Let's get her to someplace where she can cool off," Brian suggested, and picked Vicky up. The muscular man carried the limp woman out of the onsen and down the hallway to one of the bedrooms set up for the servants of visiting masters.

Josie followed behind him and pulled a black silk nightgown and matching thong from the dresser in the room. The pair quickly dried and dressed the girl, so they could put her to bed and let her sleep off the heatstroke before her master returned for her.

11

DARIEN STOOD IN THE FOYER AND WATCHED AS TIFFANY PULLED his surprised assistant away. He felt bad for abandoning her to the teen's care, but he couldn't take her in to see the Council. Tiffany would take her to Natalie, and she would make sure Vicky was put into the safety of the house pets.

Turning, he took the stairs at the other end of the room. The center stairway split at the middle into two smaller ones that led off in opposite directions. He followed the steps leading left and climbed to the grand chamber where the Council held their meetings.

"… You need to take more responsibility for those you bring over," Darien slipped into the room and waited for the Council to stop reprimanding the youngest chair holder. "You can't just turn whomever you like and let them go on the city. We've had to 'take care' of your last fledgling already."

"That's not entirely my fault," Michael defended himself. "How was I supposed to know she would try to turn all her friends, too?"

"You should have known it was a bad idea when

you found out she was a crack addict." The head council member rubbed the headache from her temple. "I still can't believe you couldn't taste it in her blood."

Michael crossed his arms and huffed at her. "Well, this time it's not one of my fledglings, Clara," he defended his brood. "I've been watching them since that last incident."

"About time."

Darien looked at the heavyset, blond man who had made the comment. That was the same thought that passed through all of their minds, but Daniel said it out loud, without holding back. Being Michael's sire prevented the younger vampire from snapping back at him.

Michael shot Daniel a look that could melt flesh from bone, but he didn't say anything.

Clara looked up from her problem and greeted their guest. "Welcome, Master Darien."

Bowing to the Council, Darien took the chair awaiting him. Even though he wasn't on the Council, they still provided a seat for him in case he changed his mind.

"We have gathered as you've asked," Clara gestured to the other six vampires sitting at the oval table. "What can we do for you?"

Darien cut straight to the chase. "I've come for information." It sounded like they were already addressing the subject he wanted to know about. Michael's coven was on the south side of Brenton, and Darien guessed that the other council members thought one of his fledglings was causing the problems there.

All seven members of the council stared at the master vampire with questioning eyes.

"Our knowledge is at your disposal," Clara offered.

"What can you tell me about the murders known as

the 'Southside Slaughters'?" Darien asked.

Michael slammed his hand onto the table. "It's not my fledglings!" he yelled.

Darien raised an eyebrow at this reaction. So, he had been right. The Council had noticed and thought it was one of their own.

"I never claimed it was one of your young, Michael," Darien used as soothing a voice as he could on the agitated vampire. "I just wanted to know what you knew about them."

Michael crossed his arms over his chest and huffed in silence.

"All we know is that there have been a series of murders and disappearances in the last few months."

Darien turned to look at the speaker, Victor. He tried not to smile at the elaborate outfit the man was wearing. Victor reminded Darien of Count Dracula in London as played by Gary Oldman, complete with silk top hat and tiny, tinted glasses. What he found most amusing was the fact that Victor had never worn these types of things until they started coming back into style with the steampunk crowd within the last forty years.

Darien turned his mind away from the man's clothing and thought about his words for a moment. "I know about the murders, but what about the disappearances?" he asked.

Lillian explained, "It hasn't been widely reported because the victims have been people no one cares about. But a lot of people have come up missing in the last few months."

Darien looked at the girl sitting cross-legged in the chair next to him. With her jeans, T-shirt, and messy, red curls, he would never have picked her out as a master vampire. "People no one cares about?"

"Mostly the homeless, hookers, and drug addicts." Lillian shrugged. "The police don't really care because there's less of a problem on the streets, but we notice."

Darien understood this. It was these types of people that vampires used for a steady supply of sustenance. Vampires would be the first to notice a drop in their population. "How many?" he asked in concern.

"Across the city?" Lillian thought for a moment. "About fifty."

He gaped at her in disbelief. Fifty people missing were a lot. "Any ideas what's happening to them?" he asked.

Lillian shook her head. "They just disappeared." Her voice held a hint of sadness. "I'd been helping out a few that have just vanished. Their stuff was where they were supposed to be, but they were not."

Darien knew that Lillian would often support a few people that were down and out to provide blood for her and her offspring. She always took good care of her people, so for them to leave without telling her was unusual.

"I was actually asked to come here today by Rupert," Darien finally revealed.

A groan sounded around the table.

"What does that mangy mutt want now?" William asked, from his seat on the other side of the table. It was clear to see the man hadn't gotten over the last conflict with the wolves.

"Apparently, the wolves have been having some trouble with the same thing that's causing the murders and abductions," Darien explained to the waiting group. "They've been chasing something they believe has caused the fires across the south, but haven't been able to catch it. In fact, the bodies that have been found torn up were all werewolves." He paused to let this fact sink into the quiet table. It was inconceivable for something to mutilate a werewolf like that. "Rupert has asked me to come and see if the Council could help."

"But… we were hoping the wolves were to blame for these actions." Clara's words were supported by an agreeing murmur from around the table. At least that would have explained part of the problems.

"No, they aren't," Darien informed them. "They're having as many problems as you are. The incidents could be related. I think it's time we put our heads together and figure out a way to stop this before it ruins life for everyone."

He was slightly surprised when agreement came from the group, expecting more resistance from the thickheaded Council.

Clara spoke for the group. "Very well, we'll put our feelings aside to find out what this is and stop it," she said. "But if it's not those mutts, and not us, then what could be causing the problems?"

Darien grinned at the way she had 'put aside' her feelings. They may agree to work with the wolves, but they wouldn't like it.

Rachel broke her silence. "It could have something to do with the Gray Courts."

Darien looked over at the timid girl. Of all the vampires on the council, she was the one he paid the closest attention to. When the quiet woman spoke, it was always important to listen.

"What do you mean?" Clara asked.

"Well, it's obvious from the extent of the damage

done that whatever is causing this is not human. That leaves things of the night. And if it's not werewolves or vampires, then the next obvious choice would be the fay," Rachael explained.

"True." William placed his elbows on the table and leaned forward. "Their powers have faded over the years as humans have taken over the wild places. Maybe this is a way for them to regain some of what they've lost? Blood magic is very strong stuff."

An understanding nod circled the table.

Daniel pointed out another issue. "But we just can't go into the Gray Courts and accuse them of these murders. We would never make it out alive."

"I know of one person who could go into the Gray Courts and ask, without endangering his life." Clara leveled her eyes at Darien.

The rest of the Council turned to the outsider as well.

Darien sighed. He knew what Clara was going to ask of him.

"Master Darien. You stand apart from all the factions. Could you take our concerns to the Fairy Queen?"

"In hopes of solving this mystery before it can escalate out of control, I'll be glad to offer my services." Darien knew this was the only way the matter would get addressed. Just the negotiations to get one of the other vampire masters into the mound might take years, and even then, the fay weren't likely to listen to them. As it was, he was in good standing with the Gray Courts and visited the Queen on a regular basis.

"Was there anything else we needed to talk about while we're here?" Clara moved the meeting on to other, in-house problems, and Darien leaned back in his chair to listen to the Council reprimand Michael for the way he treated his food.

Clara insisted that the dark ages of vampirism were over, and special care was to be shown to the 'victims' that supplied them with blood. There were occasions where death would occur from bleeding one person too much or too often, but the Council had agreed a long time ago that these deaths were to be kept at a minimum to prevent the outside world from discovering their existence. It was not this way everywhere, but Clara was a humanitarian and saw that her people followed this rule.

Some of the other Vampire Councils found this viewpoint weak and would have gladly tried for the city if it hadn't been for Darien's presence. It was clear to anyone who tried to stand against the city that Darien was truly the man in control, even if he held himself away from the politics of it.

Darien sat up and stretched as the Council broke for the evening. It had been several hours since he had arrived, and he was glad that the masters were done bickering. If it had been in his nature, he could have easily fallen asleep at the table listening to their petty squabbles.

Michael stormed from the room without greeting Darien. He had been the center of most of the complaints raised. At one hundred fifty years old, he was a master, but he acted like an overgrown kid sometimes.

"Looks like you have your hands full there." Darien smiled at the brunette who led the mismatched group of vampires. He had turned Clara a long time ago and enjoyed the fact that she had made a place for herself in the world.

Clara laughed at him. "You could always come in and take over," she offered.

It had become a running joke of theirs. Every time Darien showed up, she would offer him the Council's head seat, and he would gracefully decline it.

"No, thank you," he replied. "I would rather sit through an audit every day."

Clara laughed again. "Are you heading straight back to Brenton, or will you be spending the weekend with us?" She enjoyed the nights when Darien came out to visit. He was the closest thing to a celebrity they could get, and everyone came out to see him when he stopped in.

Darien was sure they were using his presence as a good excuse to throw a party. "I'll have to head back as soon as I can get Charlie to come out with the wrecker. I blew out a radiator hose on my car on the way over," he explained. "I had to bring my personal assistant with me, and she, well, she doesn't know about us."

Clara stopped in her tracks and stared at Darien with an open mouth. "You brought an Innocent here!"

"There wasn't much I could do about that." He defended himself. "We were in a meeting when you called, and I didn't have time to take her back to the office. She was going to just drop me off and drive back, but that was before the car broke down. I couldn't very well leave her sitting out there, waiting for Charlie, soaked to the bone."

Clara closed her mouth and thought about his situation for a moment. "You have a point," she agreed before they resumed their walk out of the council chambers. "So where is she now?"

"I ran into Tiffany on my way in and had her take

Miss Westernly to Natalie, with instructions that Miss Westernly was mine, and no one was to touch her."

Clara stared at Darien like he had made a massive mistake.

"What?" Concern bloomed in his heart.

"Tiffany's a scatterbrain these days," she said. "I hope she gave Natalie the full message."

Clara and Darien both picked up the pace. They ran down the steps and through the hall, trying to find Natalie.

"Where is she?" Darien cried, as he followed Clara into the kitchen where Natalie was baking.

Natalie looked up in shock at the greeting the normally calm man had given her. "Good evening, Master Darien. I assume you are looking for your pet?" She smiled.

Darien groaned. That just proved that Tiffany hadn't passed on his message properly. "She's not my pet," he explained. "She's my employee and an Innocent."

Shock crossed Natalie's face. "I... I didn't know!" she exclaimed.

"It's all right." Darien tried to calm himself down. "Where is she now?"

"I gave her to Josie and the house crew." Natalie found her way into one of the chairs at the table so her weakened legs wouldn't drop her to the floor. Had she known Vicky was an Innocent, she would have made sure the house crew knew to keep her away from the vampires. As it was, she had turned the poor girl loose to be dinner, without so much as a warning.

Darien pushed past Clara and jogged down the hall to the lounge. His eyes scanned the room to find all the regulars and a few vampires, but Vicky was nowhere to be seen. "Where is she?" he asked, with a note of urgency in his voice. Not all the vampires were there, and he knew the house rules said that anyone in this room was free game to all.

"We put her to bed after her bath," Brian answered.

Darien let out a sigh of relief. "Thank goodness." The tension drained from his shoulders.

"You were worried about her?" Josie asked. After listening to the way Vicky had spoken about Darien, she was sure he would be less caring.

"Of course I was worried about her. She's an Innocent."

Everyone turned shocked looks towards him.

"You brought an Innocent here?" Terrance asked from where he sat on William's lap.

"It wasn't by choice," Darien defended himself again. "The car she was going to drive back in broke down, and I couldn't just leave her to wait till Charlie came and got her. She would have caught pneumonia."

"But we thought she was your..." Jenny started, but Darien cut her off.

"No, she's my personal assistant. She runs my human life."

"But she said something about you putting someone on bed rest, and that you had been through another nine pets in the last two months!" Brian exclaimed.

Darien now understood the reason Josie had been surprised he was worried about the girl. "I'm not that kind of monster," he said, shocked. "Marianna's on bed rest because she's pregnant with triplets. And the nine women were temps trying out for the position as my assistant!"

The entire room cowered back from the power leaking off the livid vampire.

Darien closed his eyes and bit back his anger at them all. Of course they would want to ask her questions. He had never brought anyone here before. Calming himself, he tried to think of a way to salvage the situation. "She doesn't know anything about vampires," he informed the room. "What did you tell her?"

Another shocked gasp ran through the room.

"Completely innocent?" Liz asked.

Darien nodded. "She doesn't even know about me. Now, what did you tell her?"

A whistle of amazement sounded in the stunned room as he pinched the bridge of his nose, trying to fend off the headache threatening him.

"Nothing, really," Josie finally answered. "We had just started talking to her about, well, you, and she fainted from the heat in the onsen. We figured it was low blood pressure, and Brian and I put her to bed in one of the suites."

Darien let out another sigh of relief. This was not turning out to be as bad as it could have been. He looked around the room at the people that had gathered. The trickle of power that had been released during his outrage had drawn the rest of the Vampire Council into the lounge to see what had made the great man so mad. Darien noticed that everyone was there except for one face.

"Where's Michael?"

12

A GENTLE TUG ON HER HAIR PULLED VICKY FROM A STRANGE dream. She rubbed her face into the soft pillow and tried to recapture the sleep that had left her. Feeling the pressure on her head again, her eyes fluttered open. The light of the moon shown across a huge featherbed. She shifted her head as she recognized the pull of a brush through her hair.

Vicky froze for a moment as she tried to figure out what had happened. One minute she was having a weird conversation with a strange group of people, and the next minute she was having her hair brushed in bed by a stranger. Vicky went to sit up, and a hand pressed against her bare shoulder.

"It's okay, baby, relax. I'm just sorting through your hair for you."

Vicky couldn't see the man who spoke to her, but he wasn't one of the men she had been introduced to. Keenly aware of his cool hand on her bare skin, she held still, trying to decide what to do. Turning her eyes down her body, she found the shine of a black silk nightgown. She let out a sigh of relief. As long as she was wearing clothing, she could handle just about anything.

The brushing stopped, and the bed shifted as the man set the brush on the bedside table. It felt like he was lying next to her. Taking the opportunity to roll her head over, she looked at the person invading her bed.

Vicky could barely make out the well-built man in the soft, silvery light of the moon, but it was clear that he wasn't wearing a shirt. She couldn't see farther down his body, but she could feel the rough touch of denim against her leg. He had to be wearing jeans.

She tried to roll away from him, but his hand came down, stopping her escape. Vicky's eyes widened as she felt the material of her sleepwear slip around her. Yes, she was wearing clothing, but the low-cut nightgown split clear to the hip on both sides and was only held in place by thin straps over the shoulders.

"Don't go away, baby. We're just getting started."

Vicky tried to move out from under his hands as Tiffany's suggestive words came back to her. Under the right circumstances, a little uncomplicated sex was fine, but she wanted to at least know the guy's name before he made it into her bed.

"I promise not to hurt you," the man whispered as he tried to get a better hold on her.

She pushed his hands back and rolled away from him to get off the bed.

The man was faster than Vicky was. He caught her around the middle and pulled her against him. "Oh, I like them with a little fight: it heats up the blood."

She stopped trying to get away without hurting him and started struggling to get out of his iron grip.

"Feisty aren't we, baby!" The man sat up and brought her with him, pressing her back into his chest. He pinned

Vicky's hands together at her chest, and he brought his legs up around her, so she was trapped against him.

"Please, stop," Vicky begged as the man nuzzled his face in her hair.

"But you smell so good, baby."

She felt her captor draw in a deep breath from the side of her neck.

Shifting his grip on her, he pulled her loose hair back away from the right side of her face and neck. Bending her head over, he held it in place with a handful of her hair and nuzzled her behind the ear.

Vicky shivered as she felt the tip of his nose drag across the skin of her neck. "Where's Mr. Ritter?" she cried, remembering what her boss had said.

"Oh, you came with Darien?"

The breath from his words tickled across the side of her neck, making her shake. "Yes, Darien. He'll be looking for me!" She hoped this would stop her assailant's onslaught, but he just laughed against her skin.

"He can have you back when I'm done, baby."

Fear tore through Vicky as she realized this man wasn't about to stop whatever he was doing. She could feel the surge of adrenaline rush through her as she fought to get loose from his unyielding grip.

"You smell so good like that."

Vicky couldn't hold back the tears slipping from her eyes as the man tightened his grip on her hair and licked the side of her neck.

"Mmm... you taste even better than you smell."

"Please, don't!" she sobbed, as she tried in vain to stop him.

"This is going to be fantastic, baby."

Closing her eyes, Vicky prayed for the strange man

to stop. She mewed softly as she tried to figure a way out of this situation. Her eyes flashed open as she felt something hard and sharp drag across the skin of her neck. She could feel both of his hands on her, so the only other option was... his teeth.

Vicky panicked as she realized the man holding her down was going to bite her. Driven by this new terror, she redoubled her efforts to get away. The man only laughed, like he was enjoying her fear, and held her tighter. She felt the sharp points of his teeth against her neck again and let out another wordless cry as the fangs parted her skin to find their way into her pulse.

❖❖❖

"MICHAEL!" Darien yelled, as he slammed through the door where he had heard the cry from his assistant. The smell of fear, adrenaline, and blood hit him as soon as he was in the room. He met Vicky's blue-gray eyes and saw the terror they held. She was fully aware of what Michael was doing to her.

Outrage ripped through Darien and shattered away his control. That ass hadn't even bothered to roll her before biting into her.

Michael looked up from Vicky's neck to find a very livid Darien staring at him. Not the proper, reserved man that he had been told was powerful. He found a very old, very powerful vampire in full fury bearing down on him. Michael loosened his grip on Vicky right before Darien ripped him away and threw him towards the door

"Get him out of my sight before I kill him!" Darien bellowed to the people who had followed him in.

Clara and Daniel gathered the terrified vampire up and removed him from the room.

Darien turned on the bedside lamp and gathered

his limp assistant up from where she had fallen on the bed. Between the shock from the bite and the massive power he was releasing, Vicky found that she couldn't move in her boss's arms. Darien rolled her over, so he could inspect the bleeding wound on the side of her neck. He held her gently as he lowered his mouth to capture the blood leaking from the puncture marks.

Vicky gasped as she felt his tongue gather up the liquid, and a tingling warmth stopped the pain from the bite. When he placed a light kiss over the healed skin, her limbs found life, and she twisted her hands into the front of his shirt. She sobbed uncontrollably into the chest of the only person she felt she could trust.

Darien held her closer and whispered soothing, apologetic words to her as he shifted them both up the bed, so he could lean against the headboard with her wrapped in his arms.

Once they were settled at the head of the bed, Darien looked up at the crowd that had gathered just inside the door. He could feel the fear from the onlookers cowering in the darkness at the far end of the room. It had been a long time since he had released that much power, and it had been even longer since he had lost control of his temper. He sighed. If nothing else, he had reminded the vampires and their menagerie that there was a reason he stood apart from them.

Darien closed his eyes for a moment and schooled himself into a calmer state so that he didn't terrify everyone completely. Opening his eyes again, he looked down at the girl crying into his chest and patted her back softly. He glanced over the thin material of her nightgown and the way it didn't cover her legs curled under her. There was no way he was going to get the comforter from the bed over her.

"Could you please get us a blanket and some orange juice?" Darien left the question open-ended, so that anyone present could answer the call. He nearly laughed when the entire group scattered to fulfill his request.

Within a few moments, Darien was presented with three blankets, a goblet of juice, a bottle of water, and a plate of cookies. He thanked the group and had them tuck one of the blankets around Vicky, so she wouldn't get cold. The girl's racking sobs had subsided to a case of sniffling hiccups, but she hadn't moved from where she had buried herself into Darien's chest.

Darien didn't know what to do now. The little bit of blood he had gotten from Vicky's neck had reminded him that he hadn't eaten since the morning, but he could tell Vicky wasn't stable enough for him to leave her alone long enough to feed. There was no way he was going to take blood here and remind the traumatized girl that he was one of the things that had scared her. Darien's gaze fell upon the bottle of water on the bedside table with the cookies and juice. If he couldn't get blood, maybe he could trick his body into holding off the hunger by giving it something else to process until he could feed.

He turned his attention to the people still hanging around. Except for Michael, Clara, Daniel, and Marsha, the entire house menagerie and council stood in the dark, waiting for something from the pair on the bed.

"Could I get someone to open that water bottle, please?" Darien nodded to the bottle on the bedside table.

Jenny jumped up, twisted it open for him, and placed it in his hand. He thanked her as she dropped back to the place where she had been standing.

A collective gasp could be heard when Darien raised the bottle to his lips and took a drink of the water.

He suddenly felt like a circus freak show and lowered the bottle from his lips. "Do you need anything else?"

After a wave of negative answers, and the group quickly vacated the room, so Darien was left alone with Vicky curled in his lap.

Letting out a sigh, Darien drank the entire bottle of water. Now that his hunger was held off for a little while longer, he tucked the empty bottle up in the pillows and leaned his head back against the headboard to wait out Vicky's breakdown.

Vicky's mind churned as she lay in her boss's arms. She could feel him breathing and hear his heart beating, but both were much slower then she would expect from a man of his age and health. He was also much colder than any man that had held her before. But it was the blazing green eyes and the fangs that had shown in the moonlight that shocked her most. A huge chunk of her mind screamed for her to run away from him as quickly as she could, but her heart told her she was safe. Darien was nothing like the guy who had sunk his teeth into her neck. Vicky shivered at the memory, and Darien rubbed her back, gently. One word kept floating around in her brain, but she just couldn't bring herself to believe it.

Vampires were myths, legends, and the things bad romance novels were written about, not rich businessmen who ran large corporations. Vicky just couldn't bring herself to believe that her boss was part of the legion of undead. Weren't they supposed to hide in the dark and eat nothing but blood? This wasn't true for Darien. She'd seen him walk in the day. True, he didn't like sunny days, but he didn't burst into flames when the light touched his skin.

She also knew he had a passion for his coffees, and she had seen him put away an entire box of clementines in one sitting. Sure, he did look a little green afterwards and complained about heartburn the next day, but he still ate them.

Vicky sighed as she tried to wrap her head around this. A strange thought hit her, and she laughed despite the fact she was still confused and terrified.

"What's funny?" Darien asked as he patted Vicky on the back.

She pushed back from him and looked up into his face. His eyes were still a brilliant green, but they no longer held the fire that burned in them when he had first burst into the room. She was also glad to note there were no signs of sharp teeth poking from his mouth. "I think my sanity just cracked a bit," she admitted, sitting up. Vicky folded her hands and looked into the concern-filled eyes of her boss. "Are you really a vampire?"

Darien's face grew serious, and he nodded.

She let out a snort of laughter and collapsed to the bed in a fit of mirth.

Of all the reactions he had expected, laughter was not one of them. He didn't know if he should be happy that she wasn't screaming or upset that she was laughing at his status as a vampire.

Vicky looked up from where she was twisted on the bed, wiping a tear from her eye. She didn't want to tell him she found it funny that she really did have a blood-sucking boss, so she revealed the other amusing fact that shouldn't offend him. "Do you remember my friends from the club?"

"How could I forget them?" Darien smiled.

Vicky sat up as she told him about her strange friends. "While we were waiting for you to arrive, they kept pushing me for information. Since I wouldn't tell them anything, they kept coming up with some rather outrageous descriptions. One of the ideas Beth suggested was that you were a vampire out for my blood." Her right hand went up to cover the area were Michael had bitten her, and her left hand rubbed her arm near the elbow.

Darien chuckled and folded his leg up so he could lean forward to pull the hand clutching her neck away. He rubbed his thumb across her knuckles reassuringly.

"A vampire, yes. Out for your blood, no." Darien sighed deeply and dropped his head so he was looking at the blanket between them. "I am truly sorry about this, Victoria. I never had any intention of exposing you to this world."

Vicky could hear the regret in his words, and she squeezed his fingers.

He looked up into the face of his assistant.

"It's okay. Sometimes shit happens that you can't control." She smiled at Darien to let him know that she would be all right. "I've learned that there are two things you can do—deal with it and get on with life, or roll over and die. I'm not about to roll over and die. I'm not sure that I want to be anyone's snack again, but I'll get over it."

Vicky's view on life amused Darien, but her words reminded him that there was something important he needed to take care of. "Speaking of snacks…" He released her hand and pulled the plate of cookies and glass of orange juice over to her. "I'm not sure how much

129

blood you lost, but this should help."

She grinned at the offering. "This reminds me of when I used to go sell plasma." Vicky picked up a cookie and nibbled at it. "Only creepier."

Darien laughed, enjoying her odd sense of humor. "If you're okay now—" he paused so Vicky could nod at him, "—there's something I need to go take care of."

Darien withdrew from the bed and left her to enjoy her cookies and juice. When he opened the bedroom door, he found Brian leaning against the wall on the opposite side of the hallway.

"Good evening, Master Darien," Brian greeted him.

Darien stopped and stared at the guard.

"Clara sent us to see to your needs, should you call."

Darien smiled and shook his head. He should have known that Clara would post a watch. "Thank you, Brian, but I have to get something to eat."

Brian nodded and offered his wrist to the vampire.

"Have you already fed Clara tonight?" Darien asked.

Brian dropped his arm and nodded again.

"Thank you for the offer, but I'll go find someone that hasn't donated yet."

Darien started to head away when a thought hit him. He stuck his head back into the bedroom and called to Vicky. "Brian's stopped by to check on us. Would you like company while I'm gone?"

Vicky froze as she tried to remember who Brian was. The name brought to mind the polite, muscular man with wavy, brown hair.

Darien noticed the pause as she considered his offer. "I promise that he won't hurt you, but you don't have to if you don't want to."

"It's okay. He can come in," she answered. If it was

the same Brian she was thinking about, Vicky was sure it would be all right. After all, he had been so concerned for her well-being in the onsen. Maybe he could answer some of the questions running around in her head.

Darien opened the door to let Brian in. "Please make sure she's okay," he said, patting Brian on the shoulder as he passed.

Brian nodded as he slipped into the room, closing the door behind him.

Darien turned his attention to the hunger that had been growing inside of him and headed down the hall to find someone willing to give up a pint.

⬦⬥◉⬥⬦

"How are you doing, darling?" Brian asked from where he stood near the door.

Vicky looked up from her cookies at the man here to keep her company and pulled the blanket up around her shoulders again. She felt more comfortable protected inside the woven material.

"Better, I guess." Vicky admitted and took a sip of the juice, working up the nerve to ask him what she wanted to know. "Are you a vampire, too?" she asked shyly over her cookie. Brian smiled and stepped closer to the end of the bed. "No, I'm—" he started.

"—Food?" Vicky finished for him.

Brian chuckled and sat himself lightly on the end of the bed. "Sometimes." He smiled to keep the young woman from being frightened by his words. "Most of the time, though, I run the house for Clara," Brian explained. "We all have jobs here. It takes a lot of people to keep a house of this size going."

Vicky listened as she chewed her cookie. "Are the others...?" She couldn't think of a polite way to ask

131

their status.

Brian grinned and shifted to sit more securely on the bed. "We're all servants here," he explained. "Natalie is the main housekeeper. She makes sure things get done and we all get fed. I don't know if you met her, but Tiffany is her daughter."

"She was the teenager who brought me back," Vicky sat up a little more as she grew more comfortable with Brian's presence.

"Yeah, that's the one." Brian turned and pulled his legs up on the bed, so he was facing Vicky fully. He crossed them and went on with his explanation of the functions of the house. "Tiffany sometimes helps out in the kitchen or in the garden, but she's been a handful recently. And apparently, she forgot to pass on Master Darien's message, which complicated things. Natalie grounded her for it." Brian made a pained face.

Vicky snickered and took a sip from her glass. She looked down at the large wine glass filled with orange juice and held it up for Brian to see. "Who puts orange juice in a wine glass?" Vicky laughed at the absurdity of it.

"That would be Terrence," Brian replied, smiling. "He is a great guy, but he has an odd sense of style."

"So, what does everyone else do?" Vicky was starting to enjoy hearing about the weird people she had just met.

"Well, Roger is the house mechanic. He fixes whatever gets broken and keeps the onsen clean and working. Josie and Jenny keep the rest of this place clean, and Liz takes care of the gardens. Hank, well, he's the butler and public face of us all. He runs the errands and takes care of any business dealings in the real world."

Vicky took another sip of her juice as she processed

what he'd said. She was surprised that they were all just ordinary people. "What about Terrence and…" she snapped her fingers as she tried to remember the other girl's name. "Um… that gothic chick."

Brian grinned at Vicky's description. "You mean Marsha?"

She nodded, slipping another cookie into her mouth.

"They came from town with their masters, so they don't actually live here."

Vicky gave him a long 'ahhh' as he explained.

"We look out for Marsha when we can, and Terrence… well, he makes our lives interesting."

"How so?" She cocked her head, giving Brian a puzzled look.

"Well, every time William brings him over, he tries to redecorate the house in his own, how should I say… *unique* style." Brian waved his hand in front of him, trying to gather the proper words for Terrence. "He's a little… um…"

"Gay?" Vicky offered.

"Flaming." Brian laughed.

Vicky took another sip of her orange juice. Now that she was comfortable with the muscular man sitting on the bed, she worked her courage up to ask some of the scarier questions puzzling her mind. "Can you tell me more about vampires?" She spoke softly, unsure if she wanted to know the answers.

Brian tensed up a little as he thought of the best way to explain them to her. "Well, they're just normal people," he started.

Vicky scoffed into her juice.

"Okay, so they can't go out during the day, and they live off blood, and they have weird powers, and they can live for a really long time."

She giggled as the man dug himself in deeper with ever trait he listed.

He finally gave up trying to reassure Vicky. "Okay, so they're not like normal people. But they aren't the cold, heartless monsters that you see in the movies. I'm sure there are some out there like that, but Clara runs a tight ship here. She and the Council have a very solid set of rules, and they deal with anyone who breaks them very severely."

Vicky took a sip of juice to ease the sudden dryness in her mouth. She didn't know if Brian's words scared or reassured her. She pulled the blanket tighter around her and opened her mouth to ask questions about the person she *really* wanted to know about, but she was interrupted by a loud knock on the door.

Brian and Vicky both looked up to see the door crack open and two heads pop in.

"Can we come in?" Jenny asked.

Vicky nodded and Jenny and Josie hopped up on the other side of the bed. Shifting back to give them space, Vicky set her plate on the bedside table.

"How are you doing, sweetie?" Jenny asked as she looked over the younger woman wrapped up in her blanket.

"Better," Vicky said. After talking with Brian, she was feeling a little better about the whole ordeal.

"We were talking about vampires," Brian informed the new arrivals about their conversations.

"We're so sorry." Josie leaned forward and touched the edge of Vicky's blanket. "If we had known, we would *never* have left you alone like that."

Vicky reached out of her blankets and took up the

blonde's hand. "It's okay," she said, squeezing Josie's hand reassuringly. "It's not your fault."

Josie smiled weakly and pulled away, sitting back up.

"Where is everyone else?" Vicky asked and looked towards the door. If these three had come down, would the rest of the group follow?

"The Council has gone to bed. It is almost dawn," Jenny informed her.

Vicky looked towards the window to see the night starting to fade.

"As for the rest: Terrence is with William, Marsha is with Michael, and Roger is sacked out on the couch in the lounge…"

"As usual." Brian rolled his eyes.

"…and Liz is seeing to Master Darien."

Vicky unconsciously raised her hand to cover her neck when she heard the name Darien had yelled. "Michael was the one that bit me." She shuddered a little as fear gripped her heart, and a tear formed in the corner of her eye.

"It's all right, darling." Brian shifted up the bed so he could touch the blanket wrapped around Vicky. She dropped her hand down and took up the offered comfort. "You're safe now."

Vicky tried to smile and nod her head, but it didn't really work.

"I can promise that Michael won't touch you again," Jenny added. She snorted out a harsh laugh. "He is well and truly terrified right now."

Vicky's eyes widened as she turned towards Jenny.

"As he should be," Brian added with a satisfied note.

"We're all a little terrified right now," Josie swallowed and looked over at the door. The scene from earlier played in her mind. "I've never seen Master Darien that mad before."

"And that power!" Jenny shivered. "I've never experienced anything like it."

Vicky released Brian's hand and pulled her blanket tighter as she listened to the three people talk about the man who had just saved her.

"That wasn't normal?" Vicky asked. Brian, Josie, and Jenny all looked at her with shocked faces. She gave them a 'how should I know' shrug.

"Not for any vampire I know," Brian explained. "Master Darien is kind of a mystery to us all."

"We were always told that Master Darien refused a Council seat a while back, but I always thought it was because he had paid the Council to leave him alone," added Jenny.

Josie shrugged. "He doesn't come around here very often. That's why we were asking you about him."

"I only ever see him at work," Vicky offered. "And he's never given me any reason to think he was a vampire."

Vicky's three visitors looked at each other in confusion.

"Never?" Josie asked.

"Well, there was that one time with that woman, but I figured he was just trying to intimidate her." Vicky shrugged again. "But, that would explain his bad habit of only having coffee for lunch."

"Wait, lunch? As in, at-noon-type lunch?" Jenny asked. "You work during the *day?*"

"Isn't that when most businesses are open?" Vicky asked with a hint of sarcasm in her voice.

The look of pure shock on Jenny's face made Vicky want to explain. "I report to work at seven AM, and we work till we're done. Sometimes, rather late in to the evening."

Brian tried to wrap his mind around this. "Where do you work?"

"Top floor of the main building downtown. There's a magnificent view of Main Street from Mr. Ritter's office windows." Vicky sat up a little. She was proud of her job.

"He has *windows* in his office?" Josie asked, like this was an outrageous idea.

"Yes." Vicky didn't understand why this would be a foreign concept to the group. "But we don't spend much time there." The group let out a sigh of relief that Vicky still didn't understand. "Mr. Ritter is always running around, making sure the various ends of his business are running smoothly. Why, just the other day we were out for the groundbreaking ceremony for the new shipping hub."

Jenny gasped. "I read about that in the paper! It was in the afternoon!"

"Yes, it was at three," Vicky confirmed.

"But how did he get out into a field at three in the afternoon under the sun?" Jenny asked.

"Um... he wasn't happy about it, but we walked," Vicky explained. The gaping faces told Vicky that this was out of the ordinary for vampires "That's... not normal," she stated in a very flat voice.

"No, that is *not* normal," Jenny confirmed, as soon as she collected herself. "The masters aren't subject to the rise and fall of the sun like the fledglings are, but they can't get out and move in the daylight."

"Clara can get out a little on very cloudy days, but she burns under strong sunlight," Brian added. "And she's the oldest here at around five hundred fifty."

Vicky whistled in amazement.

"How old would Master Darien have to be to handle full sun?" Josie asked.

"Nine hundred years," Darien answered from where he stood, leaning against the door that Josie and Jenny had forgotten to close.

Brian fell off the bed trying to turn around and see the man who no one realized had joined them.

"Although, I started to be able to really get out at around seven hundred," Darien added as he walked into the room.

Brian scrambled from the floor where he had fallen and circled the bed to stand behind Jenny and Josie, gawking at the vampire coming into the room.

Darien let out a sigh. The only person who wasn't bothered by his presence was the one person not use to vampires.

Vicky watched as Darien tucked one of his hands in his pocket and crossed the room to stand next to her. She felt odd seeing her well-dressed boss rumpled after the long night. His expensive dress shirt was wrinkled in the front from where she had clung to it, and he had rolled the sleeves up to his elbows. His silk tie was missing, and he had unbuttoned the top two buttons of his shirt so he was more comfortable, but it was the smear of blood on the front of Darien's shirt that made her turn her gaze away, embarrassed. It was too dry to have happened recently, so it must have gotten on him while he was holding her.

Darien picked up a cookie that had fallen from the plate. He took it with him to go lean against the wall and stared at the people in the room. "Is there anything else you want to know about me?" Darien asked as he raised the sugary snack to his lips and took a bite.

Josie, Jenny, and Brian stared in an awed silence as they watched the vampire consume the wayward treat. A million questions swirled through their minds, but they were all very personal and inappropriate to ask.

"Are you really nine hundred years old?" Vicky asked, looking back up at him.

Darien shrugged. "Give or take a little. They didn't keep very good records where I was born." He popped the other half of the cookie into his mouth and dusted off his hands.

"Where was that?" Vicky asked.

Brian's eyes widened at the woman's audacity. These questions were not something one asked a master vampire.

"Glendalough, County Wicklow, Ireland," Darien answered.

Vicky thought about this for a moment. "If you're Irish, why don't you have a cool accent?"

Darien laughed at her question. "I find that it's easier to pass as a local without it, cailín."

Vicky's eyes widened at the rich, Irish lilt he slipped into.

"Now, if we are done with the inquisition, it has been a long night, and I think we could all do with a little rest."

Darien pushed away from the wall and placed his hands on Vicky's shoulders. Josie and Jenny both slipped from the bed as he pulled Vicky to her feet and stood her next to the bed, wrapped in the blanket. Pulling the covers back, he moved her back into the bed properly. Darien made her lie on her side, facing the middle of the mattress, and he pulled the duvet up to tuck her in.

Vicky's breath caught as she felt his fingers pull

through her hair and tuck the loose ends behind her ear. His fingers caressed her locks as he bent over her. She was sure he was going to kiss her on the cheek when she felt his breath on her face.

"Sleep," Darien whispered into her ear.

Vicky's eyes closed as the suggestion stole the tension from her body. Within seconds, she had fallen into a deep and restful slumber.

He caressed her hair one more time before turning his attention to the three people watching silently from the other side of the bed. "I suggest you get some rest, also." The Irish note was gone from Darien's voice as he patted his sleeping assistant one more time. "Unless you need to be tucked in, too."

Brian, Jenny, and Josie took this as a hint to get out and vacated the room before Darien could make good on his offer. They hadn't felt any trickle of power when Darien had put Vicky to sleep. Either she was very susceptible to suggestion, or he was just that powerful. Either way, they didn't hang around to find out.

Darien sighed deeply at the speed with which the three visitors left. By the time he woke up, his story would have been shared with the rest of the house. He really didn't mind that, but it meant that the entire place would walk more softly around him for a while. Of course, last night's little outburst of power hadn't helped matters, either.

Darien let out another sigh and opened the window at the far end of the room. Taking a deep breath of cool, morning air, he dropped himself into the overstuffed armchair next to it. Crossing his ankles on the matching ottoman and folding his hands across his stomach, he relaxed back into the soft cushions, letting his consciousness slip away for a much-needed rest.

13

VICKY YAWNED AS SHE WOKE FROM THE MOST RESTFUL SLEEP
she'd had in a long time. Shaking away the last of the
cobwebs in her head, she sat up in the bed. The soft sent
of lilacs filled the room, and she looked around for the
source of the smell. Her eyes found the open window
at the other end of the room before shifting to the man
sleeping in the chair next to it.

Vicky smiled at how cute her boss looked, sacked
out in the chair, with his head bent forward onto his
chest. The afternoon sun sent a beam of light to dance
on his lap, just below his hands. She slipped from the
warm covers to close the curtains, so the light wouldn't
touch his skin. He could handle the little bit of sun, but
she knew that Darien made a habit of avoiding it if he
could. Now she understood why. It was the least she
could do for the kindness he had shown her last night.

Vicky moved as quietly as she could, so as not to
wake the sleeping vampire. Now that she stood next
to him, she looked down at his unmoving body intently.
After watching Darien for a full minute to see that he
drew no breath, Vicky was half tempted to touch him

to make sure he was still alive. Deciding to leave him be, she went to the door on the other side of the room. She was glad to see her suspicions were correct, and it was a rather large bathroom.

After quickly relieving herself, Vicky stood in front of the vanity mirror as she washed her hands. She stared at her reflection in the mirror for a long time. Even though her world had changed, she still looked the same. The wound on her neck was completely healed, and the only trace of the incident was the blood that had dried on her chest and the front of her nightgown.

Wetting a washcloth, Vicky wiped away as much of the dried blood as she could, thinking about her predicament as she worked. What was she going to do? Her boss was a nine-hundred-year-old vampire, masquerading as a human. She paused in her scrubbing and looked at herself in the mirror as she came to a conclusion. It didn't matter that he was a vampire. He was still her boss, and she really did enjoy her job. This only added to his eccentricity. Shutting the water off, she dried her hands and headed back to the bedroom to see if she could find something more appropriate to wear.

Vicky opened the bathroom door to find that Darien had left while she was washing away the blood. He had pulled open a few drawers on the bureau and the doors on a wardrobe before leaving. Curiosity drew Vicky to the open wardrobe, and she found it contained a variety of clothing in a range of sizes. It took her a moment to find some jeans and a shirt that would fit. She borrowed them from the closet and tossed them on the bed. Searching through the open drawers, she found an assortment of undergarments. Taking some out, she added these to the pile on the bed.

It didn't take her long to change out of the soiled nightclothes and into the clean garments. Vicky picked up the brush left on the bedside table and shuddered as she remembered what had happened the night before. She recalled Sue's advice and pushed the memory of the bite away. Now that she'd had time to think about it, Vicky was determined not to let the incident overshadow the rest of her life. She quickly sorted through her sleep-rumpled hair before slipping out of the bedroom and wandering down the hall, barefoot, in search of someone who could point her in the direction Darien had gone.

It didn't take Vicky any time to realize that the hallway outside the bedroom was the main hall and would connect her to the onsen, the lounge, the kitchen, and finally, the foyer. She made a quick stop in the changing room of the onsen to see if she could find her shoes, but the basket where she had left them was empty.

Next, she headed into the room where she had met everyone last night, but no one was there. Puzzled by the lack of life in the house, Vicky headed back down the hall to the kitchen. She found several plates with food on them, but no one was in there, either. Her stomach growled at the smell of food, and she snatched up a blueberry muffin from a stack before heading back out the door and down the hallway to the foyer.

She could hear voices coming from the open front door, and she walked over to see what the excitement was about. The entire menagerie was standing in the doorway, gaping at Darien as he tried to get Roger to look at the Torino.

"It'll take Charlie three hours to get here with the wrecker," Darien explained to the astonished man. "Can you fix the damn car or not?"

Vicky giggled at the awed look on Roger's face as he tried to pull his attention away from the vampire standing in the sunlight to look at the car. Slipping past the shocked residents, she went to save her frustrated boss.

Vicky danced across the hot concrete, only stopping when her bare feet found the cooler ground in the shade of the car. By the time she made it, Roger had actually gotten the hood open and was trying to look under it.

"I think they're just surprised to see you out here, Mr. Ritter. I'll take care of this." Vicky patted her boss on the arm. "I'm pretty sure I saw a fresh shirt in the closet in that bedroom. Why don't you go get cleaned up?"

Darien looked at her, then down at the wrinkled, bloodstained shirt he was wearing, and snickered. "All right, Miss Westernly, but let me know if we have to call Charlie. He's going to kill me if I've torn up one of his babies." He turned to go back inside.

Vicky watched as the crowd at the door parted to let the vampire back into the house. She laughed as they followed him inside in amazement. Turning her attention back to Roger looking at the doorway where Darien had just disappeared, she prodding the mechanic back to work. "Close your mouth and check out the car."

Roger snapped his mouth shut and turned his attention to the machine in front of him. "I didn't just see that, did I?" he asked the woman next to him.

She pulled the paper off one side of her muffin and picked at a blueberry. "What, a twenty-three-year-old woman ordering a nine-hundred-year-old vampire around? Or said vampire walking around in the sun?" she asked, nonchalantly, before nibbling the berry she had pulled from her pastry.

"Both," Roger gaped at her.

"Yes, you did. Now can you fix the car?" Vicky took a bite of the muffin while she waited for him to get himself together enough to check out the problem.

Roger shook himself and looked at the engine of the car. "This is a really nice car." He twisted the cap of the radiator off and peering in it to see that there was no water inside.

"It'll do the quarter mile in 13.99 seconds at 101 miles per hour." Vicky rattled off what she'd heard Darien tell Mr. Rodgers yesterday day. It got her the same appreciative whistle from Roger that had come from the shipping hub manager.

"That's hot!"

"Right now, it's got a busted radiator hose," Vicky explained.

Roger dropped to the ground to check out the damage. "What is this?" he called from under the car. In a few moments, he sat up on the driveway, holding out the remainder of the stockings that had been wrapped around the hose. They were dirty and slightly burnt, but it was obvious what they had been at one point in time.

Vicky swallowed to clear her mouth and tried to remain unaffected by his find. "You act like you've never seen a pair of stockings before."

Roger looked up at the girl curiously.

"What?" she said, defending her choice of repair material. "It worked to get us here."

He dropped the ruined silk to the ground and stuck his head back under the car. "Well, the radiator hose is cracked," he called from under the car.

"Tell me something I don't know," Vicky sassed back at the man.

Roger chuckled at her. He wasn't sure she was the same shy woman they had met last night. "I should be able to get a replacement at the parts store in town." He pulled himself up from under the car and shut the hood. "I just need to know the year and model of the car."

"It's a 1970 Ford Torino." Vicky got another appreciative whistle from Roger.

"That's going to be a hard order to fill, but I think I know just the guy who would have what I need."

"Good. Please let me know how it goes," Vicky answered very professionally.

"Do you want these back?" Roger picked up the stockings and held them out to her.

"No. You can keep them if you like," she smirked.

Roger grinned and turned to head back to the house with the damaged stockings in his hand. He had only walked a few steps before Vicky sprinted past him across the hot driveway. He looked back over his shoulder to see what had caused the woman such haste. Unable to see anything unusual, he turned back to find that Vicky had reached the shade of the porch and was rubbing the bottom of one of her bare feet into the calf of her opposite leg, trying to soothe the tender skin.

"Where are your shoes?" Roger asked as he mounted the steps to the porch.

Vicky looked up from inspecting her foot. "No idea."

"You should've said something. I would have been happy to carry you back."

Vicky cocked an eyebrow at him. "Are you hitting on me?"

"I would never dream of it." Roger smiled as he spoke.

She rolled her eyes at the sarcasm in his voice. "Let me know when you have an answer on the car." Vicky laughed as she turned back into the house. She was hungry, and that muffin had not been enough.

Roger sighed and went to go make some calls.

Vicky made her way into the kitchen to find that the abandoned plates had once again been claimed by their owners. Stopped in the doorway, she was unsure if she should enter and disturb the host talking excitedly around the table. It surprised her to find that almost everyone had gathered in there, discussing what they had just witnessed.

"How is that even possible?" Terrance waved his fork around as he talked. "I mean, it's five in the afternoon and not a cloud in the sky!"

"Any of the other masters would be in trouble if they tried that," Liz said as she stirred the beef stew around on her plate. "I nearly died of shock when he stepped out into the light."

"She said he could walk in the sun, but I really didn't believe it." Josie shook her head as she tore a hunk of bread up and dipped it into her gravy.

Natalie looked up from her plate at the new addition to the room and almost knocked over her chair as she stood. "Victoria!" she cried, and the rest of the room fell silent.

Startled by the woman's outburst, Vicky instinctively took a step back.

Natalie rushed to her and took her hand. "I am so sorry."

Vicky's eyes widened at the unexpected apology.

"I didn't know, or I would never..." She patted the

Vicky's hand and smiled apologetically.

"It's okay," Vicky said reassuringly.

Natalie looked at the younger woman for a moment before pulling her into a tight hug.

Vicky returned the embrace to show there were no hard feelings.

When Natalie finally released her, she stepped back and looked at Vicky. "You must be starving." She pulled the younger woman into the room, placing her in a chair at the table

"We're sorry, too," Liz said as she tapped her spoon on the bottom of her dish.

Natalie set a plate of the same beef and vegetable mix in front of Vicky.

"It's okay," Vicky reassured her. "I'm not upset."

Liz nodded and dug back into her stew.

Marsha squished a carrot with her spoon and looked up at Vicky, slightly remorseful, as if she wanted to say something but didn't know how to go about it.

Vicky took up her spoon and dipped it into the thick gravy. She stirred it around before taking a bite. "This is very good," Vicky complemented Natalie's cooking.

She thanked Vicky and went back to eating her own food.

Vicky could tell that her presence made the group a little uncomfortable because they didn't return to the conversation they had been having. They ate in an awkward silence, until Roger came into the room and reclaimed his chair.

Roger looked over at Vicky. "I found what I need to fix your car." He rubbed the back of his neck as he talked. "The guys should be delivering it within the hour." If Roger had noticed the heavy air in the room, it didn't show.

"Thank you," Vicky answered as soon as her mouth was empty. "Mr. Ritter will be happy to know that we don't have to call Charlie out to pick us up."

"Who's Charlie?" Roger asked, as he sat forward to start into what was left of the meal Darien had interrupted.

"He's the guy who takes care of all the cars," Vicky explained. The rest of the table watched her intently as she spoke. This was more information about the enigma that was Darien.

"What types of cars does he have?" Roger asked between bites.

Vicky shrugged. "All kinds. He's got some new sports cars and several classic cars, but you'll need to ask Mr. Ritter for details. I really don't know much about them. But, he takes the classic ones out once a week to show them off." Vicky scraped another bite from her plate and stuck it in her mouth.

"Do you really work during the day?"

Vicky looked up at the odd question from the other end of the table.

Embarrassed, Marsha turned her face away.

"Yes," Vicky replied. "From seven AM till whenever Mr. Ritter is done."

Marsha looked up and met Vicky's gaze. "Does he really eat and drink food?"

Vicky could see the disbelief in her eyes. "I have seen him eat and drink many things," she answered, and a murmur of astonishment circled the table. "Mainly coffee and clementines."

"And you really didn't know he was a vampire?" Liz asked.

"No." Vicky could see the amazement in the faces around the table as she answered. "Up until last night, I thought vampires were B-rated horror movie fodder."

"There are some really great vampire movies out there."

The entire table turned to look at Darien as he walked into the kitchen with Clara.

Vicky's heart skipped at the sight of her boss dressed in jeans and a T-shirt. His damp hair hung messily onto his face.

Darien shook it back and ran his fingers through it, so it would stay out of his eyes. "Some of them fall way off the mark, but they're still entertaining."

"But, there are also some really bad ones out there," Vicky pointed out.

"Too true," Darien laughed and dropped himself into the empty seat next to Vicky.

"Good evening, Miss Westernly."

Vicky looked up at the woman who had come in with her boss.

"I am Clara, the head of the Vampire Council."

Clara was fair-skinned with mousy, brown hair that hung neatly to her shoulders. Vicky studied her hazel eyes, but she could not find anything that screamed vampire.

"I would like to apologize for your ill treatment last night. I have had words with Michael, and he asks that you forgive his misconduct."

Vicky's hand strayed to her neck as she listened to the woman speak.

"I assure you that you are safe here for the remainder of your stay, and in the future, if you choose to return. You are welcome here at any time."

"Thank you." Vicky smiled and stood up to shake Clara's hand. "I would gladly come back."

Clara smiled warmly at her guest.

"Have you heard anything about the car, Miss Westernly?" Darien asked as he eyed the plate of stew Vicky had been working on.

Vicky turned to address her boss. "Roger said he was getting the parts delivered from town within the hour." She sat back down and picked up her spoon.

"It should only take me about thirty minutes after that to get her up and running," Roger said around a mouthful of food.

Darien nodded his approval. He could feel the eyes of the other occupants in the room on him. Placing his elbows on the table, he picked up a roll and toyed with it. Darien tore a bit off and rolled it in his fingers. A smile curled the corner of his mouth as he dipped the bread into Vicky's gravy.

"Do you mind?" Vicky scowled at the invasion.

"No," Darien smirked, as he popped the gravy-laden bread into his mouth, earning him a gasp from the rest of the room.

Vicky rolled her eyes and went back to her food. It was easy to see that he was showing off.

Clara sighed. "You're going to make yourself sick," she said as she circled the table and took the chair next to Brian.

"I haven't done that in a long time." Darien chuckled as he bit off another piece of the bread. "Anyway, I like the taste of food and have always wanted to try Natalie's cooking." He chewed for a moment before turning his attention to the cook. "It's very good."

Natalie blushed and thanked him.

"When you're done grandstanding," Clara sniggered from the other side of the table, "why don't you show Miss Westernly around?"

"That's an excellent idea, Clara," Darien answered. He popped another piece of the roll in his mouth.

Clara quickly broke the tension that had settled on the room by prodding Liz into a description of the gardens.

⊷⊶❂⊷⊶

"Wow, these are really beautiful roses," Vicky commented, sniffing at the large blooms surrounding the gazebo. She had gladly gone with her boss on a tour of the mansion after their meal.

Darien stood in the shade of the trellised outbuilding and smiled over the magnificent garden that Liz had showered with love. Being a vampire's home, Liz had picked a healthy mix of plants that would bloom during the day and at night. Darien had seen the wonders of Liz's garden under the full moon, but this was the first time he had the pleasure of walking in it during the day. He had always tried to avoid doing things that would make Clara's people wary of him, but the events of the last day had pretty much blown those plans out of the water.

Vicky glanced up at Darien gazing over the lush foliage of the English-style garden, and pondered what she had learned. She watched him stick his hand out on the railing, where the sunlight sparkled, and pull it back into the shade. He did this several times as he admired the handiwork around him.

"Are you really a vampire?" Vicky asked as she watched him.

Darien looked over at the odd question.

152

"It's just... you're nothing like I ever dreamed a vampire would be." She shrugged.

An odd grin turned up the corner of his mouth as he played with the sunbeam.

"I assure you that I am a vampire and have been everything your imagination can come up with, and more." He looked out over the garden again as he remembered evil things from his past.

Vicky blanched as her mind came up with some very nasty things she had seen in some movies.

"I've done some very dark things in the time I've lived." Darien looked back at his assistant. "But most of it's in the distant past. Still, you should always be wary when dealing with vampires, no matter who they are."

Swallowing hard, she thought about his words. She looked away from his serious expression and down to the hand flitting between sunlight and shade. "Does it hurt?"

"What?" Darien was confused by the question.

"The sunlight." She pointed to the beam Darien was playing with. "I thought sunlight was supposed to hurt vampires."

He looked down at his hand and smiled. "Yes, the light used to burn when I was younger." Darien rubbed his hand where the sun had been touching. "Now, it's like the angry bite of electricity. More uncomfortable than painful." He looked back at Vicky. "I'll still burn under strong light. That's why I don't go out during the middle of the day if I can help it."

"So... no sunbathing," Vicky teased.

The corner of Darien's mouth turned up in amusement. "No."

"If vampires are real, what other... um..." She

stopped before she could use the word that had popped into her mind.

"Monsters?" Darien offered, as if he was reading her thoughts.

Vicky's eyes widened at the word. "I wasn't going to use that word."

"Maybe not, but it fits. We've all done some monstrous things." Darien looked back over the garden. "A lot of the myths of the world are based in truth. Stories of vampires, werewolves, fay, witches, and even demons are all real. Sometimes the facts get twisted up in the retelling of the tales, but you should still heed a warning from all of them. What one would call *supernatural beings* walk among humans every day. We hide what we are to avoid persecution, but I can guarantee that you know many such creatures, without being aware there is anything special about them. Those that can't hide have withdrawn into places where human society cannot endanger them."

Darien let out a sigh before he went on. "The sad part is the most monstrous things done in all of history were done by normal humans. The creatures of the night try to keep a low profile so they can go on living their lives without worry."

"You haven't kept much of a low profile," Vicky pointed out. "You're one of the highest-profile people I can think of!"

Darien smiled at her. "True, but how many people know I'm a vampire?" He raised an eyebrow, and she nodded her concession. "Anyway, even if someone named me for what I am, how many people would believe them?"

"You have a point," she admitted and looked out

over the garden again. Vicky could hear the roar of the Torino's engine starting in front of the house.

"Sounds like Roger's done." Darien approached the steps that would take him out of the gazebo. "Maybe we should go check it out."

Vicky nodded. "Then we can find where my clothing and shoes went to," she said and padded after her boss, barefoot.

Darien chuckled his agreement.

A smile curled the edges of Darien's lips as he looked over at his assistant. Vicky was slouched over in the seat so her head rested against the window of the car. He shook his head as he studied the long line of unguarded skin down the side of her neck. He had warned her to be cautious around all vampires, yet, here she was, sound asleep and utterly defenseless in his company.

Darien placed the tip of his finger on the soft spot behind her ear and pulled it down so that his nail scraped softly across the pulse point in her neck. Vicky moaned lightly in her sleep and rolled her head back, so the skin stretched a little more. He rubbed his finger back and forth on the bit of clavicle exposed by the cut of her shirt as the hunger stirred in him. The tips of his fangs press into his lip, and he could still taste the sweet tang of her blood from when he had licked it from her wound last night.

Pulling his hand away, he gripped the steering wheel tightly and looked out at the street in front of Vicky's apartment. With a long-practiced ease, he pushed the hunger away and recomposed himself. No matter how easy or tempting she made it, taking Vicky's blood was the one thing Darien would not do. She had proven herself very capable in her job, and drinking from her would only complicate things more than they already were.

"It's time to wake up," Darien said as he reached back over and touched her shoulder. He shook her just a little.

Vicky yawned as sleep released her. She sat up, rubbing her eyes, and yawned again before looking over at her boss.

"Have a nice nap?" Darien asked with a smile.

She nodded and rubbed the side of her neck where his nail had left a slight red mark on her skin. "Sorry." Vicky apologized for passing out as she stretched the stiffness from her limbs.

"It's all right," he reassured her. "You've had a very busy day. I suspect you'll be tired for the next day or two."

Amusement slid across Vicky's face, and she shook her head as she remembered highlights from her day.

"Go get some rest."

"That sounds like a great idea." She gathered up the plastic bag containing her work clothing. Someone at the mansion had cleaned and folded them up for her. Slipping back into her heels, she pulled the messenger bag over her shoulder before opening the door to get out. "Have a nice night, and I'll see you on Monday, Mr. Ritter," she said as she stepped out of the car.

"Good night, Miss Westerly," Darien replied as she shut the door and headed into her apartment building. He waited for a moment to make sure that she was safely inside before he left.

He was surprised at how strong a person Vicky was. She seemed to handle being tossed into the middle of his world pretty well. Either that, or she was in an amazing state of denial. Darien decided it would be a wise idea to teach her more about what was out there. As she became more aware of the supernatural things of the world, they would start to take a greater interest in her. They could really cause her problems if she wasn't properly prepared for them.

❦❂❦

Dropping her bags on the couch as she passed, Vicky kicked her shoes off. She was glad to be back in the relative safety of her home. This entire weekend had left her with a lot to think about. After checking the time, she decided it wasn't too late for a nice, relaxing bath. It would give her a chance to reflect.

Vicky stopped up the drain and added some rose-scented bubble bath to the gurgling water. The soft scent reminded her of the roses outside the gazebo in Liz's garden and the conversation she'd had with Darien about other 'monsters'. He'd assured her she knew others pretending to be human.

Sitting on the edge of the tub, Vicky trailed her fingers through the growing bubbles as she thought of all the people she knew. Could any of them be something other than human? The only person she could think of was the biker-like man who had stopped into Darien's office just over a week ago. Vicky shook that thought away and stripped off her borrowed clothing, so she could slip into the fragrant water of her bath.

Vicky turned her mind to the people she had met at the Vampire Council. The only person there who didn't seem bothered by Darien's strangeness was Roger. She had watched the way the other members of the menagerie, and a few of the Council members, skittered around her boss when he walked into the room. But Roger wasn't intimidated at all. He had happily engaged Darien in a lengthy conversation about the vampire's car collection while making playful passes at Vicky. This had earning him several scalding looks from Jenny.

"Don't mind him, sweetie," Jenny said, as she patted Vicky on the arm. "He's incorrigible."

Vicky had laughed at this. She could feel the tension in the group lessen as the two men talked on about cars. It was just the balm needed to soothe everyone's frayed nerves. It was only when Vicky turned to find Daniel clamped to Josie's wrist that her fears had been renewed. She'd quickly excused herself to go to the kitchen. She needed some water to relieve the dryness that had suddenly come to her mouth. Daniel had finished by the time Vicky came back, but it wasn't long until Darien announced that it was time to leave. Clara had offered them her hospitality until tomorrow, but Darien had refused because he needed to get back for some unfinished business.

Vicky suspected that Darien could feel her unease with the vampires. They all seemed to be very nice people, but she wasn't sure she was ready to hang out with them yet. She was still a little unnerved by the sight of fangs poking out of a few of their mouths. Vicky sighed and turned off the tap, so she could relax back into the hot water.

Closing her eyes, she thought about her boss. She had definitely seen fangs when he had rushed to her aid, but that had been the only moment. The rest of the time, his teeth had been quite normal. She had spent a better part of the evening pondering how he hid them. Darien would probably tell her if she inquired, but it felt rude to ask. And frankly, she wasn't sure she wanted to know the answer.

She thought about confiding in her best friend about her issues, but she was sure that was a bad idea. First, Darien wouldn't want his secret getting out, and second, Vanessa would think Vicky had gone crazy.

Vicky wasn't sure she was still wholly sane as it was. How could vampires be real? Were there really legions of undead out there, mingling with normal people, just waiting to suck out their blood? If they *were* undead, what animated them? How did one become a vampire? These and many more questions bounced around inside Vicky's skull.

Sighing, she shook her head to clear the unanswered questions from her mind. If she hadn't fallen asleep in the car, maybe Darien could have answered some of them. As it was, the drone and gentle vibration of the car had combined with her fatigue to lull her into a restful slumber. A yawn slipped from Vicky as she relaxed in the water. She could feel the tired ache slipping from her as she rested in the hot bath. Leaning her head back onto the edge of the tub, she let her mind drift away to think of things on its own accord.

"You should always be wary when dealing with vampires, no matter who they are," Darien whispered as he moved towards Vicky.

She stood just in front of the master vampire. A light burned deep in his green eyes, and she could clearly see the tips of his fangs between his parted lips. Vicky wanted to heed his warning and run, but she couldn't move.

As he wrapped his arms around her, Darien reached

up and pushed her hair back, exposing her neck. Using one long finger, he tipped her head over ever so slightly, before drawing his nail down across her pulse point. He ended by rubbing the ridge of her collarbone, revealed by the low cut of her sundress. Holding her tighter, Darien leaned his face down to her throat. Panic bloomed in Vicky as she felt him place a light kiss on the side of her neck.

"This is going to be fantastic, baby."

Adrenaline shot through Vicky's veins as the man holding her changed from her trusted boss into Michael. She screamed as he sunk his fangs into her again.

⋘•O•⋙

Vicky splashed a large amount of the tepid water out of the bath as she thrashed free of her nightmare. She sat up and looked around her bathroom for the man who wasn't there. Wrapping her hand over her neck, where the dream vampire had sunk his fangs in, Vicky squeezed herself with the other arm. After a moment of deep breathing, she relaxed and pulled the plug to let the cooled water out.

She got out and wrapped herself in a towel. After pausing in the doorway to make sure no one was in her apartment, she sprinted into the kitchen. A quick searched of the cabinets revealed a partial bottle of Jack tucked away from Vanessa's last visit.

Opening the bottle, Vicky sat down on the floor to take a long pull. The whisky burned down her throat as she curled forward to hug her legs to her chest with her free hand. She took another mouthful of the liquor before setting the bottle on the floor. Rubbing her temple with her hand, she tried to push the memories out of her mind.

The nightmare had brought back last night's escapades in living color, and she considered calling Darien for comfort but pushed the thought away. She was a grown woman and should be able to handle a simple bad dream on her own. Vicky took another slug of the alcohol before twisting the cap back on the bottle. She was starting to feel the warming effects it was having on her body. Standing up, she hid the bottle away in the cabinet before heading to her bedroom.

She dropped the wet towel to the floor and wrapped herself in her favorite nightgown before burrowing into her comforter. It felt safe swaddled in her blankets. One eye and her nose poked out from under her covers as Vicky studied the pattern on the kimono and tried to push the nightmare away. When her heart rate had finally slowed, Vicky let out a deep sigh and relaxed, letting sleep take her away.

"WILL THERE BE ANYTHING ELSE, MR. RITTER?" VICKY ASKED AS she stood before Darien's desk.

Darien looked up from the file she had just handed him and studied his PA. She was smartly dressed, as usual, but he could see the tiredness around the edges of her eyes. He dropped the file to the desk and folded his hands on top of it. "How are you doing?"

Vicky was slightly surprised by the concern in her boss's voice. She looked into those deep, green eyes and considered talking to him. Twice in the night, she had woken up from nightmares about being bitten. Deciding that it was her problem to deal with, she smiled at her boss.

"I'm fine," she tried to lie.

Darien scowled at the untruth.

Vicky quickly amended her statement. "I just didn't sleep very well."

His expression lightened slightly. Darien could tell she wasn't telling him everything, but he knew what was bothering her and saw no point in pressing the information from her. "All right," he conceded, and watched as Vicky let out the breath she'd been holding. "But let me know if there is anything I can do for you, Victoria."

Touched by the concern in his voice, she answered, "I will."

"Good," Darien approved. "There is one other thing you could do for me." He paused, waiting for Vicky to pull herself back to the right frame of mind before continuing. "I want to go over this before my next meeting." Darien patted the file under his hands. "Could you please make a run to the café for me?"

"No problem." She nodded. "Your usual?"

"No, ask Sue for something special."

Vicky cocked a curious eyebrow at her boss but didn't ask. Hopefully, the young barista would understand Darien's request. "I'll be right back."

Darien picked up the file and poured himself back into it as soon as she left.

"Good morning, Miss Westernly." Sue smiled as Vicky walked up to the counter. "The usual?"

"For me, yes, but Mr. Ritter asked for 'something special'."

Sue paused at the odd request. Concern flashed through her, but she tried to hide it from Vicky. "Coming right up!" Sue chirped cheerfully.

Vicky gave her a weak smile before turning her attention to the room behind her. The café sat just off the main hallway, so people were always passing by. She watched each person, wondering if they were human or something else.

"Is everything okay?"

Vicky was startled back to reality as Sue set the

drinks on the counter behind her. "I've had a really weird weekend," Vicky answered. Her hand rose to cover the healed vampire bite unconsciously.

Sue's eyes followed the telltale motion. "Did he bite you?" she asked softly.

Vicky's eyes nearly popped out of her head. "What?" she asked, shocked.

"Master Darien. Did he bite you?"

"No, it was someone else..." she began. "Wait! You know Mr. Ritter is a..." Vicky stopped, not wanting to say the word out loud.

"...A vampire?" Sue finished for her. "Yes, I know."

Feeling her knees weaken, Vicky looked around for a chair to sit in before she fell over. She backed up and took a seat at the table next to her as the shock stole the rest of the strength from her legs.

Sue hurried around the counter to make sure Vicky was all right.

"I'll be okay," she reassured the concerned girl. "I'm just a little overwhelmed by it all."

Sue retrieved the coffees from the counter and handed one to her. "Why don't you tell me about it?" Sue offered as she sat in the chair next to Vicky. "Maybe it would help to talk."

Vicky looked up at her reassuring smile and started into her story. Sue listened intently as Vicky relayed their trip out to the Vampire Council. She pursed her lips as Vicky recounted Michael's behavior, but she smiled when she heard about the way Darien had thrown the man and tended to Vicky. Sue was spared no detail as Vicky spun her story. She even included the nightmares plaguing her.

Sue sat and considered what to say to the upset woman. "You don't have to worry about anything with

Darien around."

Vicky looked up at the reassuring words.

"He won't let anything else happen." Sue smiled warmly at her. She could still see the fear in Vicky's face, so she went on. "Darien's reach is much further than you think. The vampires now know you are under his protection, and no one else would dare to touch you while you're carrying that," Sue pointed to the bag Vicky had slung at her hip.

Vicky was surprised to find it there. She hadn't realized that she had picked it up on her way out.

"The werewolves have already been warned about to you."

"What?" Vicky stared at Sue in disbelief.

"It's true," Sue informed her. "Darien's had words with the local pack alpha, and he's made sure the rest of the pack knows who you are." Seeing the shocked look on Vicky's face, Sue decided it wouldn't be a good idea to reveal that, since Rupert's little misunderstanding, he had been sending wolves to make sure Vicky got home safely every evening.

"But how do they know who I am?" Vicky looked around as if someone was watching her.

"That bag marks you as being Master Darien's." Sue spoke softly to try to ease Vicky's nerves. "Even if you didn't have it with you, you've spent enough time in Darien's company that you're starting to smell like him."

Sue giggled as Vicky raised the back of her hand to her nose and sniffed it. As far as Vicky could tell, she didn't smell any different from normal.

"It would take a much keener nose than yours to detect the change," Sue informed her.

"How can you tell?" Vicky asked as she lowered her

hand from her face.

The barista smiled again. "I have a much keener nose."

Vicky's eyes widened in surprise.

"I'm a werewolf."

Vicky gawked openly as she processed this fact. She couldn't believe that this sweet girl was one of the monsters Darien had warned her about.

"You mean like fur and fangs in the full-moon light?" Vicky said in disbelief.

Sue laughed out loud. "I've never heard it so elegantly put, but yes." She smiled warmly.

A million questions rushed into Vicky's brain. "But how do—"

"There you are." Darien called as he finally located his assistant.

Vicky's mouth slammed shut on her questions. "Mr. Ritter!" she gasped instead and turned towards him, shocked that he had come looking for her. Tearing her eyes from the unexpected sight, she found the clock on the wall and realized she had been gone for much longer than she intended.

Vicky jumped to her feet as Sue stood up and took the drink she had made for Darien.

"Let me refresh this for you, Mr. Ritter." She smiled again at Vicky before slipping back behind the counter.

"Did you have a nice chat with Sue?" Darien asked, smiling at the color that rushed across Vicky's cheeks.

"I'm so sorry, Mr. Ritter!" she exclaimed. "I didn't realize it had gotten so late."

Darien placed a reassuring hand on her shoulder. "It's all right. We still have time before the meeting."

Vicky let out a relieved sigh when her boss didn't reprimand her.

"Do you feel better now?" he asked.

She looked up into his concerned eyes and thought about the question for a moment. Sue had given her a lot more to think about, but the fear and worry that had been troubling her were gone. "Yes, I think I do," Vicky answered.

Darien nodded his relief and dropped his hand away from her shoulder.

"Here you go, Mr. Ritter." Sue placed a fresh drink on the counter.

"Thank you, Sue." He picked up the drink and took a long pull from it. He turned his attention to Vicky. "If you are ready to head out, I need to go yell at the board about these numbers. They are way off the mark this month."

Vicky smiled and nodded her head. "Thank you, Sue," she waved to her friend.

Sue waved back. "Any time."

Vicky grabbed up her coffee and followed Darien, who was leading the way to the boardroom. She was surprised at how quickly she had gone from dealing with the supernatural things slipping into her world to listening to her boss complain about figures and monthly spending reports. Sighing, she turned her mind back to her job.

Darien paused in his rant to drain the rest of his drink, so he could dispose of it in one of the large trashcans in the hallway. It wouldn't do to take the cup of blood into the meeting and risk it being dropped into one of the smaller wastebaskets. He licked the last drops from the plastic cover before tossing it in the can.

Looking back at the woman following him, he pushed the button to call the elevator. Once they were both inside, he watched the reflection of his assistant in the shiny surface of the door. Vicky had plucked one of the shoulders of her shirt up and was sniffing at the collar. A thoughtful look crossed her face, and she smoothed her shirt back into place. "What are you doing?" Darien asked as he turned to look at the odd behavior.

Embarrassed, Vicky took a slight step back as she realized she had been caught in her investigation. "Um..." She couldn't think of a good explanation, so she went with the truth. "Sue said I was starting to smell like you."

Darien looked at her for a moment before closing the distance between them.

Vicky tried to retreat from him but found she was already against the back wall of the small, enclosed space. He placed his hand on the wall next to her and bent his head to the crook of her neck. Her pulse raced as Darien swung his face across her shoulder and up the side of her head. She could hear the deep intake of air as he pulled in her scent. Her breath hitched as he pushed away from her, and she met his eyes. His pupils were significantly dilated from where they were when he had first trapped her.

"So you do," Darien confirmed.

Vicky's heart skipped again. Before she knew what happened or had the chance to act on the strange impulses being sent from that tight pull in her gut, he was back over by the door where he had started.

"I hadn't noticed."

Vicky wanted to laugh hysterically at how calm her boss was after doing something so intimate and inhuman.

In all honesty, Darien was very affected by the trembling mess he had made of his assistant. He smiled to himself as she pulled herself together. He loved the way she smelled and was sorely tempted to offer her a place in his menagerie. It had been many years since he had kept what some of the Council called "pets," but the sight of Michael with his fangs in Vicky had stirred something in him that Darien hadn't felt in a long time.

Darien had become keenly aware that he was starting to have feelings for his assistant. Vicky's presence brought something to his life that he hadn't known he was missing. The smile that lit up her face, her innocence, the fact that she kept bringing him clementines. These had all moved him in ways he hadn't realized until she was in danger. Darien had thought about it over the last day and decided the best thing to do was to wait. If Vicky handled this change in her world well, maybe he could invite her in deeper, but he wasn't going to do anything that would endanger her ability to act as his PA. She did an excellent job, and he would be hard-pressed to find someone to replace her if she quit. Darien reached for his calm center, trying to push away all thoughts of the woman trapped in the small box with him. He took a deep breath to clean out his head but found that the air was filled with scents. Her rose and jasmine perfume, a touch of fear, a hint of desire, her natural smell, and his own rich aroma mingled to form a heady mix that tugged at his body. Holding his breath, he could school himself back into a business mindset. He still needed to whack around the heads of his board members who were getting out of line. When the elevator door opened, he was glad to see Vicky had also recomposed herself and was ready to take on the challenges of the rest of the day.

15

Vicky shut her front door and turned to drop herself over the arm of the couch. She stared up at the ceiling and tried not to think about what had happened that day. After the incident in the elevator, Darien's attitude was strictly business as usual, and they ran on through their day like nothing had happened. She shook her head. Maybe this was normal for vampires. Surely, it wasn't the strangest thing she had seen him do, and it wasn't as if he had actually touched her. He just smelled her in the most provocative fashion in which she had ever been sniffed. Vicky blushed as she remembered the feel of his face against her hair and the look in his eyes.

Shuddering, she pushed the intense image away. She needed something to distract her, and she knew just the thing. Vicky rolled off the couch and found her cell phone in the bag. She had started carrying her own things in Darien's messenger bag. It was just easier to carry one bag instead of two. Hitting a number on speed dial, she waited for the phone to connect.

"Hey, Vicks," Vanessa's voice echoed down the line. "What's up?"

Vicky smiled at the familiar sound of her friend. She was sure that Vanessa was human. "I was just wondering if you wanted to go out tonight?"

"That would be fantastic!" Vanessa squealed. "Beth just told me about a special event over at Alchemy. I thought about asking you, but seeing that it's Monday, I didn't think you would want to go."

"As long as I don't stay out too late, it's fine," Vicky answered.

"Fantastic! Do you still have that black velvet dress you got at the Crystal Fair?" Vanessa asked.

Vicky thought about it for a moment. "You mean the floor-length one with the wide, pointed sleeves?"

"That's the one!"

"I think it's in a box under my bed. Let me look." Vicky got up and headed to the bedroom to check. She pulled out a plastic tub containing clothing she didn't wear but couldn't throw out. "Yes, it's here." She pulled a long, stretch-velvet dress from the box and placed it on the bed.

"Great! Beth and I will be over in thirty minutes to help you with your makeup."

Vicky could hear Vanessa bounce as she spoke.

"Get out those heeled boots from last Halloween. This is going to be great!"

Vanessa hung up before Vicky could ask what was going on. She sighed and went to take a shower before her friends showed up.

⋘◦⋙

"I'm not so sure about this." Vicky looked at her reflection in the mirror.

Beth and Vanessa had curled Vicky's hair so that it fell in rolls down her back. They had used a foundation that whitened her out, a light pink lipstick, and very heavy eyeliner. Coupled with the black dress and black vinyl boots, she looked like she could be a poster child for Hot Topic. All she needed to do was dye her hair black, and the image would be perfect.

"I think you look fantastic!" Beth sprayed the last length of hair, so the curl would stay. Pulling the iron away, the curl bounced down with the rest of them. "All done," she said.

"Not quite," Vanessa said, retrieving something black from her bag. She wrapped the wide strip of a velvet collar around Vicky's neck. "Now we're ready."

Vicky examined the necklace in the mirror. The inch-wide collar was adorned with two red crystals set a smile's width apart. From the back of each crystal hung three chains, each tipped with a blood-red jewel. The six droplets danced across Vicky's collarbone. Her heart skipped as she looked at the simulated vampire bite sitting over her pulse point.

"I can't wear this." She lifted her hand to remove it.

"But it's perfect!" Beth complained as she stopped Vicky from touching the collar.

Vicky sighed deeply at her friend's stubbornness. "You still haven't even told me what is going on at Alchemy tonight." She eyed the corset Beth was wrapped in.

"It's Goth Night!" Beth squealed in excitement.

Vicky looked over at the pirate costume Vanessa was dressed in.

"It was the best I could come up with on such short notice." Vanessa shrugged as she settled a tricorne hat on her head.

Vicky had wanted to go clubbing to get her mind *off* vampires, not go hang with humans pretending to *be* them. She sighed and shook her head. Loud music and dancing was still loud music and dancing, no matter what the atmosphere. "All right," Vicky acquiesced. "Let's go before it gets too late."

Beth bounced in delight, and the three friends stopped long enough to pick up Beth's steampunk jacket from the couch. Vicky slung the messenger bag over her shoulder.

Beth frowned at the bag. "Why are you bringing that thing?" It was ruining the line of Vicky's dress again.

"I told you last time." Vicky grumbled at her friends as she opened the door. "I'm on call and have to have it in case Mr. Ritter needs it."

"So you're at his beck and call?" Vanessa laughed.

Vicky blushed at the lewd implication. "It's not like that," she hissed, locking the door behind them.

"I'll gladly be at his beck and call," Beth said breathily as she thought about Vicky's boss. "He's hot."

"Stop it," Vicky hissed again, causing her friends to giggle. "I don't want to think about him that way. He's my boss." The incident in the elevator popped into her mind, and she was glad it had started to get dark. It made the red on her skin harder to see.

"Does he work you too hard?" Vanessa teased, and Beth giggled.

Vicky let out an exasperated sigh and grinned at her teasing friends. "Sometimes," she said, and her girlfriends oohed at her. She rolled her eyes and covered her face as they went into all the ways they would like her boss to work them.

"You two are perverts," Vicky sighed, as Vanessa parked her car in the lot next to the club. "Now, would you cut it out so we can dance?"

Vicky tried to calm the heat from her skin, but there was no way she was going to get rid of the smile cracking across her face. Both Beth and Vanessa had very active imaginations, and the two girls had come up with a plethora of perverted things as they drove to the club.

"But, we were just offering suggestions you could try out the next time you're alone with Mr. Tall, Dark, and Handsome," Vanessa teased.

More like Mr. Tall, Dark, and Fangy, Vicky thought to herself. "Please, I just want to forget Mr. Ritter for the moment and have a good time," Vicky begged her friends.

Beth and Vanessa could see this topic was starting to bother Vicky, so they dropped it. "Let's go pick up some hot guys who can't fire us," Beth teased, and the three girls crossed the parking lot and disappeared into the thumping music issuing from the club.

The empty bottle clinked against the table as Vicky set it down and went to stand at the edge of the dance floor. Her eyes found her friends mixed into the crowd, swaying to the music. Vanessa had one guy pressed to her back and another rubbing against her front. The guys' pirate costumes were identical, and they seemed to be twins. From the action on the floor, Vicky was sure those two scurvy dogs were going to steal her ride home tonight. Vicky's gaze kept wandering until they found Beth hanging out with the steampunk crowd. She had a guy wrapped around her, and they were grinding on the dance floor.

Sighing at her lack of luck, Vicky stood at the edge of the floor and swayed in time to the music. There had been several men who had started her way, but all of them had been intercepted by someone else, or they turned away before they reached her. She looked down at the formfitting dress she was wearing. Yes, it was long, but it hugged her in all the right spots. She shook her head as she tried to figure out why her luck was so bad tonight. Normally, she could find at least one person willing to dance with her.

She was just thinking about getting her fourth beer, when she felt a hand on her hip.

"You would be surprised to know how many phone calls I got, telling me you were here."

Vicky looked up at the familiar man pulling her into the line of his body. "Mr. Ritter!" she squeaked, completely shocked that he was standing in the thumping club. Too astonished to pull away, Vicky let Darien lead them back to the table where she had been sitting.

He placed her in one side of the booth and waved at the waiter for two more beers before sitting down opposite her. "You look very nice tonight," Darien complemented her.

Vicky was still too dumbfounded to think as she looked over her boss. She couldn't believe that he was in a dark, peasant shirt and black leather pants with a lace-up fly. The ends of the pants were tucked into black, knee-length plainsmen boots held in place by a cord wrapped around them. His rich, brown hair was artfully messy and hung into his face. Vicky gawked at the roguish air rolling off her boss as he lounged back in the booth. One arm was stretched across the back of the seat as the opposite leg kicked out across the opening of the booth. It wasn't far enough out in the aisle that someone would trip over it, but it did prevent Vicky from an easy escape if she chose to run. Her mouth flapped as she tried to respond, but nothing came out.

Cocking an eyebrow at her, Darien worked to keep his amusement off his face. Their bubble was broken when the waiter set two bottles on the table. Darien nodded his thanks, and the waiter made himself scarce.

Vicky took a swig from the bottle Darien slid in front of her. "What are you doing here?" she finally found her voice as she looked at her boss in surprise.

Darien picked up his bottle by the neck and took a sip of the ale. "I told you. I got several calls telling me you were here by yourself, so I came."

Vicky gawked at his words. "I'm not here by myself," she informed him, "I'm here with Beth and Vanessa."

He looked back at the dance floor, where Vicky's friends were hidden. "I see." A smile cracked across his face as he took another sip of his beer.

Vicky huffed at him and crossed her arms over her chest. "I usually have better luck than this." Relaxing, she picked up her beer again and looked out at the sea of men who refused to dance with her.

"I have to apologize to you for that one." Darien looked a little guilty. "It's not because you don't look nice, I assure you. You look ravishing by the way."

She squirmed in her seat. "Thank you." She took another sip of beer to cover her unease at having his eyes on her. Once the drink was clear of her mouth, Vicky voiced the thought that popped into her head. "If it's not what I'm wearing, then why is everyone avoiding me?" She looked up at Darien. "What did you do?"

"Nothing." He chuckled. "I didn't have to do anything."

Vicky cocked her head, pondering his words.

He could see the confusion in her eyes, so he went on to explain. "Goth Night is when the vampires and their minions hit the clubs."

She whipped her head around to look at the throng of people gyrating on the floor.

"Most of them are either vampires or have some connection to vampires."

Swallowing hard, Vicky raised her hand to her throat as she thought about his words. "Will my friends be okay?" she asked as concern filled her.

"They'll be fine," Darien snickered. He had already spoken to the masters in the room to ensure that her friends were off the dinner menu for the evening.

She sighed with relief. "But that still doesn't answer why I couldn't find someone to dance with." She pouted in her beer.

Darien chuckled again and took another sip. "They're afraid of me," he whispered. Vicky's eyes widened a little at this.

"I'm sure every one of them has heard about the incident this past weekend. That's why none of them have approached you. They're under the impression that you belong to me."

She gaped at him again. "But I *don't* belong to you!" Vicky objected.

"True." Darien sipped his drink again as he explained. "You are your own person and do as you please, but I have offered you my protection. Twice. First, with the werewolves, and now, with the vampires. These people see life by a different set of rules. Since I have given you my protection, they view you as mine and off limits."

"Well, there goes my social life," Vicky huffed and slouched back into her bench.

Darien tilted his head to look at her thoughtfully as a smile slipped across his face. "Only if you plan on dating a vampire or werewolf."

Vicky picked at the label on her bottle as she thought about this. Sitting up, she took another drink of her beer and looked back out at the people populating the club. Now that she was looking at the crowd more closely, she could see eyes watching them. The owners of those eyes still danced and chatted with their partners, but their attention was focused on the master vampire drinking beer in the booth. Laughing out loud, Vicky dropped her head to the table to giggle herself silly.

Shocked by this reaction, Darien sat up to make sure she was all right.

She rolled her head over to look back out at the crowd once her mirth subsided. Sighing, she sat up to talk with Darien again. "I actually wanted to go out tonight to get my mind off everything," Vicky admitted as she took another sip. "It was Beth's idea that we come out for Goth Night. I never expected to run into a..." she waved, looking for a name for the large group of vampires.

"It was originally called a murder, but you can call it a kiss," Darien offered.

Vicky gave him a confused look. "A murder?" she asked.

"It comes from the name for a flock of crows," he explained.

"Oh." Vicky filed this bit of trivia away and went back to what she was saying. "I never expected to run into a kiss of vampires." She took another pull on her beer. "Is this going to happen every time I go out clubbing?"

"No," Darien replied. "It's true that vampires and their crews run the clubs, looking for those willing to donate blood, but they usually don't come out in the numbers here tonight. Goth Night at any club is seen as a chance for the different broods to get together and mingle."

Vicky nodded as he educated her.

"Vampires are a common theme in gothic culture, so it's not an unusual topic. That's why we can sit here and chat about vampirism so openly."

"So, no Goth Night." Vicky nodded, making a mental note.

"Not unless you want me to come with you," Darien added, toying with his beer bottle. "You may also want to avoid raves. Those tend to be the preferred hangout of the werewolves."

Vicky's eyes widened, and she drained the rest of the beer from her bottle.

Darien took the empty bottle away from her and pushed his partial beer towards her. "I'm not going to finish it," he explained as she looked at the offered drink.

She shrugged and rolled the bottle between her hands. She was drunk enough that she wasn't going to let some swapped germs bother her. "Thanks for coming out and explaining things." Vicky swirled the beer around in the bottle before taking a sip. "I'm sorry if I pulled you away from anything important."

"Nothing that needed my attention." Darien grinned. They sat in silence for a while as Vicky picked at the label on her bottle. Darien leaned back in his booth and sighed. "It's still fairly early in the evening, and you came out to dance, so why don't you go have a good time? I'm sure you'll find someone to dance with, now."

She gawked at him again. "I can't leave you sitting here by yourself," Vicky gasped at the idea. "It would be rude."

"I'll be fine," Darien waved her concern away. "Besides, this isn't my type of music."

Vicky sat staring at him for a moment, torn. She did want to get up and dance, but she didn't want to leave him by himself.

Darien moved his leg back so she could get out of the booth without falling over it. "Go. Have a good time." His words were gentle, but the command in them left no room for argument.

Taking one last pull from her drink, Vicky slipped from the table.

Darien relaxed back into the booth and watched the hem of her dress swirl around her feet as she headed to the dance floor. She stopped at the edge of the wooden surface and looked back at him one more time.

He shooed her on, and she stepped into the mass of people and disappeared into the writhing bodies. Darien could feel the asking eyes of the other vampires in the room. He nodded his approval before leaning his head back and losing himself to the thumping rhythm of the music. Watching through half-lidded eyes, Darien smiled. He could understand why Vicky would choose such a place to unwind. The heavy beat was almost primal, yet relaxing to the mind.

As soon as Vicky stepped onto the dance floor, she was swept away by the movement of the crowd. Before Darien had shown up, the crowd parted when she came out to dance. Now it engulfed her. Vicky felt the soft touch of fingers shepherding her farther onto the dance floor. She never saw the hands or their owners in the mob around her, but they led her to the center of the floor. Closing her eyes, Vicky gave herself over to the music, and it didn't take long to get properly lost in it. When she opened her eyes back up, she found herself in a group of six of the hottest guys on the floor.

Vicky was bombarded by a barrage of dance partners, each one dancing with her for a few moments before handing her off to the next. After reaching fourteen, she stopped counting and just enjoyed the movement of the crowd. The faces that passed by, gave her something to think about. Some of them had fangs, but Vicky wasn't sure if they were real or costume. Surprisingly, they didn't bother her in this setting as much as she thought they would.

Thought of vampires and her feelings towards them bubbled around in her head as she was passed from person to person. The grasping hands of her next partner ripped Vicky from her thoughts. Instead of catching her waist like the others had, he grabbed her ass and ground her against him uncomfortably. Gasping at the course action, she moved to push away from him, but she was swept from his grasp before she could do anything.

A rich tenor echoed from the chest Vicky found herself buried in. "You do not treat Master's Lady that way."

Looking up into the face of the man who had saved her, the fangs were the first things she noticed, but they didn't look out of place in the handsome face framed by long, blond hair.

"Are you all right, my dear?"

Nodding, Vicky stepped away from him, and swayed slightly as the alcohol caught up with her.

"Easy there." The blond man grabbed onto her shoulder to save her from falling over. "Maybe we should get you back to your master." She eeped as he pulled her in against his side and turned towards the booth where Darien was sitting. The crowd parted before them as he walked her off the floor.

"But he's not my master," Vicky protested weakly. She wanted them to know she was her own person.

The man grinned. "That may be so, but it's obvious you belong to him." He patted her hip where his arm was wrapped around her. "Consider it a great honor... Master Darien hasn't kept a companion in a very long time."

Vicky wanted to protest, but they had arrived back at the table where Darien was sitting.

"Elliot!" Darien smiled up from where he lounged in the booth. "I didn't know you were back in town." He stood to shake the man's hand.

"Good evening, Master Darien. I only just arrived," Elliot answered as he took ahold of the offered appendage. "I found something that belongs to you." He released Vicky and spun her around to stand next to Darien. "She was being accosted on the dance floor."

Darien looked over the girl at his side and wrapped his arm protectively around her shoulders.

"Don't worry. She is well, and the problem has been dealt with."

He nodded his approval. "Thank you."

Elliot bowed at Darien's words. "I think it would be wise to take her home," he said, offering his advice. "It's getting late, and she's a little drunk."

Vicky huffed at him, but she couldn't argue with his point. Now that she wasn't lost to the music, she was feeling the alcohol. "Fine," she agreed. "But I need to let my friends know that I'm leaving."

Stepping away from Darien's side, she stumbled a

little and was saved by two pairs of hands as the vampires employed their speed to catch her before she fell.

"Thank you," she muttered as her skin flushed.

"Let us help you." Elliot whirled around to take her arm. Darien took the other, and they walked Vicky out to the floor.

She looked back over her shoulder at the booth. "My bag!" she protested.

"I have it here." Darien patted the bag on his hip.

She let out a sigh of relief and allowed the two men to take her to find her friends. The crowd parted, and Vicky could see several people bow to them as they passed.

It didn't take long to find the first of Vicky's friends hanging out with the steampunk group. Beth and her dance partner stilled as the two vampires escorted Vicky over.

A man dressed in a velvet-trimmed, Edwardian morning jacket stepped out of the group to greet them. He bowed slightly to Darien. "Master Darien."

"Master Victor." Darien returned the greeting.

Vicky looked between the two master vampires before stepping away from her escorts to talk with her friend still held captive by her silent dance partner. "I'm heading home, Beth. I have to work in the morning," she explained.

Beth nodded to her but was looking over Vicky's shoulder at the two handsome men who had brought her over. She stared at them with her mouth open.

"*Beth.*" Vicky prompted.

"Yes!" Beth snapped her mouth shut and turned her attention back to her friend. "Um… going home. Yes. Then we need to find Vanessa. She has the car." Beth stumbled over her words as she tried to put her brain in gear.

Vicky giggled. "You look a little preoccupied." She smiled at the man still wrapped around her friend. "Why don't you stay here, and I'll go find Vanessa." Beth just stared at her and her escorts as Vicky and the men turned to go find Vanessa.

"Don't worry about her," Elliot winked at Beth before he turned away. "She's in good hands."

Beth's mouth worked in a way that would make a goldfish proud as she tried to come up with something to say. She had never seen Vicky pick up two hot guys in one night.

They found Vanessa still pressed between the pirate twins. When Vicky approached, the men paused before moving to stand next to each other behind the woman Vicky was looking for.

The twins bowed slightly to them. "My Lady," they greeted her. "Master," they greeted Darien.

Vicky didn't know why, but she dropped into a curtsy as Darien bowed to the pair.

"Jakob. Josh." Darien greeted them.

Vanessa stared at who was behind Vicky. Wrapping an arm around Vicky's, she pulled her friend away from the men following her. "Is that your boss?" Vanessa whispered to her best friend.

Vicky nodded.

"What's he doing here?" she hissed as she looked back over her shoulder at the handsome men.

"It's a long story," Vicky said with a sigh. "I'm heading home. It's getting late, and I have to work in the morning."

"Do you need a ride?" Vanessa asked as she peeked back over her shoulder at Vicky's boss.

A smile turned up Darien's lips as he heard the implied meaning behind her question.

"I'm fine," Vicky answered. She was sure that Darien intended on taking her home. "You stay and have fun."

Vanessa giggled. "Oh, I plan on it."

Vicky looked up at the two men waiting for Vanessa to finish with her friend. Since they had greeted Darien, they had to have something to do with the vampires. Concern colored Vicky's thoughts for a moment, but she pushed it away. Darien had assured her that her friends were safe. "I'll see you later." Vicky hugged Vanessa and turned back to the two men waiting for her.

"I'll call you about this weekend!" Vanessa waved to her.

Vicky raised a hand in response.

The pirate boys were back on Vanessa before Vicky could get totally away. She shook her head at the giggles issuing from her friend. Only Vanessa could find a set of twins to entertain her for the night. Vicky pushed that thought away and let Elliot and Darien lead her off the floor and out the door.

They stopped just outside the club, and Darien turned to the other man and nodded his thanks. "Are you staying in town?" he asked.

"Yes, with some of Rachael's fledglings," Elliot informed him. "If you need anything, please call me, my liege." He bowed deeply and swept his hand across his chest in a very old-fashioned manner.

Darien nodded very slowly.

Elliot stood up and turned his attention to Vicky. Taking her hand, he bowed over it. "It was a pleasure to meet you, My Lady."

She blushed as he placed a kiss on the back of her

hand.

"I look forward to our next meeting."

Unsure of the proper response, Vicky muttered another 'thank you' as Elliot released her and disappeared back into the club.

Darien took her by the arm and led her through the parking lot to his little sports car. "What's going on this weekend?" he asked as he slipped Vicky into the passenger seat of his Aston Martin. He handed her the messenger bag, and she laid it on her lap.

"It's girls' night out with the old dorm crew," Vicky explained as Darien settled himself into the driver's seat.

"Do you always come out to Alchemy?" He started the car and backed out of the parking space.

Vicky shrugged and looked out the window. "Most of the time. We used to go across town to Red Jack's, but some guy wouldn't leave Maggie alone, so we found another club. I have to say, I like Alchemy better."

Darien smiled at this. He was good friends with the owners and had financed the club when it first opened. "How often do you go out with your friends?" he asked, maneuvering the car into traffic. When Vicky didn't respond, he looked over to find that she had fallen asleep against the door again. Darien chuckled and turned back to the road in front of him. He was amazed at how comfortable she was in his company, even after she knew what he was.

Darien parked his car in front of Vicky's building and looked over at his sleeping assistant. The two red crystals on her collar teased him, sparkling just above her pulse point. He shook his head and pulled on her shoulder, so she wouldn't fall out when he opened the passenger door. Vicky moaned lightly in her sleep but didn't wake up.

He got out and circled the car to open her door. Slipping the messenger bag from her lap, he fished in it to find her keys. House keys in hand, Darien slung the bag over his shoulder and bent to lift the sleeping girl from his car. With Vicky secure in his arms, he kicked the door shut before turning to take her inside. She snuggled into his chest and sighed contently in her sleep. Darien smiled softly at the woman and soon had her up the steps and into her apartment.

Making his way into her bedroom, Darien held her tightly to him as he dropped her legs to the floor. With his free hand, he pulled the bedding back before lifting his drunken assistant into her bed. He took a moment to remove her shoes before making sure she was properly tucked in. Brushing her hair away from her face, he looked down at the black collar that had been teasing him.

"This is very apropos for tonight's venue," Darien whispered as his fingers found the clasp at the back of her neck and pulled the velvet band off. "The next time you want to sport a vampire bite, all you need to do is ask." He looked down at the two marks on her neck from where the chains attached to the back of the collar had pressed into her skin. Bending over, he placed a light kiss over the mark and drew in the soft scent of her skin. "You make this much too easy," Darien whispered against her neck and stood back up.

He checked to make sure Vicky's alarm clock was set and turned to head out. His eyes landed on the kimono hanging on her wall, and he laughed out loud. "Sleep well, Victoria," Darien patted her legs on his way past.

Darien made sure the door would lock itself before he deposited the bag and her keys on the couch and left. It would be in his best interest to have someone he trusted watch out for Vicky when she went partying with her friends. Twice now, they'd left her to fend for herself at the club, and Darien didn't find them very trustworthy. He thought about who would be best to send as he got back into his car and went to find dinner.

16

Vicky looked up from her desk at the tall man walking into her office. She raised her hand to her neck as she recognized the same dark-haired man who had accosted her two weeks ago. Swallowing back her fear, she stood to greet him. "Good afternoon," she said as firmly as her voice would let her. "May I help you?"

Rupert was surprised that Darien's PA wasn't cowering in the corner. He could smell her fear, but she was doing a remarkable job of hiding its outward signs. "I'm here to see Darien Ritter." Rupert stopped in front of the desk and smiled. "I have an appointment today."

Vicky ran the schedule she had committed to memory, and pulled the man's name out... "Rupert Marshal?" she asked, to confirm.

"At your service," he bowed politely.

Vicky cocked her head at the odd response. "Please have a seat, and I'll let Mr. Ritter know you're here." She waved the man to the chairs against the wall. Turning away from Rupert, she knocked on Darien's door. When no answer came, she opened it and poked her head in.

"I don't care what excuse you've come up with,"

Darien spoke sharply into the phone. "I don't pay you for excuses; I pay you to do your job. Either get it done or I'll find someone else."

He looked up from where he was listening, and Vicky signaled that his four o'clock was there. Darien looked at the clock on his wall and nodded. He signaled he wanted some coffee, and she nodded and left as he snapped into the phone again.

She turned back to the man studying the pictures on the wall between the chairs. "Mr. Ritter is on the phone at the moment," she informed him, pulling her bag from under her desk. "He'll be with you as soon as he's done." She slipped the bag over her shoulder and settled it on her hip. Gathering up her courage, she stepped around her desk and into the open space next to the werewolf. "I'm heading out to get some coffee for Mr. Ritter. Would you like something?"

Rupert was awed by how polite she was to him. "Black coffee, please," he said, accepting her offer.

Vicky nodded and made her way out of the office.

Rupert watched her walk past him with a calm facade. He stood there, looking at the doorway for a full minute, until Darien came out of the office.

"Good afternoon, Rupert," Darien greeted the pensive werewolf.

"You have a very interesting assistant." Rupert stared at the door where Vicky had disappeared.

Darien laughed. "That she is."

"I don't know what I was expecting," Rupert turned to face Darien, "but she seems well-composed."

"I'm sure she was terrified of you," he reassured the alpha. "But, after the weekend she's had, you don't seem that scary." Darien held out his hand to lead Rupert into his office. "Come on inside, so we can talk."

Rupert headed through the open door. "I heard something happened with the vampires, but my sources didn't say what."

Darien closed it behind them.

"I also heard you were out at Alchemy on Monday."

Darien chuckled at the werewolf.

"Terrifying the fledglings?" Rupert teased.

"Not intentionally." Darien sighed. "Miss Westernly's friends decided it would be a good idea to go out for Goth Night, and they took her with them."

"Had to go save your minion?" Rupert grinned.

"Hardly." Darien circled his desk so he could sit down, while Rupert took one of the leather armchairs. "I had to go reassure the young ones that I wouldn't kill them for touching her." He shook his head.

"They haven't been that afraid of you in *years*." Rupert pondered this fact. "What'd you do to scare them so badly?"

"I took Miss Westernly with me to the Vampire Council over the weekend." Darien rubbed his temple as he spoke. "There was an incident with Michael."

Rupert raised an eyebrow.

"He bit her," Darien explained.

"And he's still alive?" Rupert asked in surprise.

"Things got complicated." Darien shrugged. "If my instructions had been passed on properly, and he had still bitten her, he'd be dead."

"He's an ass, anyway." Rupert shook his head. "We have more problems out of his broodlings than all the other masters combined."

"I know it." Darien shook his head and remembered that more than half of the council meeting had dealt with Michael and his flock. Switching topics, he asked, "Have you had your pack following Miss Westernly?"

"Um..." Rupert looked away from the vampire. "...for her safety, yes."

"I thought I smelled wolf on her the other day."

"Phelan caught her last Thursday, when she nearly fell into the street," Rupert explained. "Some idiot was biking on the sidewalk, and Miss Westernly caught her heel in a grate trying to get out of his way."

"That's good." Darien nodded his approval. "You may want to warn your wolves that she knows about their existence now. Sue's been helping her deal with the changes in her world."

Rupert nodded. "Sue's a good person to talk to. She's the best sister I could ever have."

"I definitely appreciate her work." Darien smiled. "Do any of your people hang out at Alchemy?" He moved the conversation on, again.

"Yeah, Zoe and Mitzy are there every weekend. Why?"

"Miss Westernly and her college friends hang out there every now and then," Darien explained.

"You want them to call you when she's there?" Rupert offered.

"Nothing that extreme." Darien waved the offer away. "I'm just not too sure about her friends. They've abandoned her both times I have seen them hang out," he explained. "I just want to make sure someone is around to help if something should happen."

"Some friends," Rupert huffed, and Darien nodded. "Don't worry about the lass. I'll make sure the girls know to keep an eye out for her."

"Thank you." Darien turned the conversation again.

"I suspect you would like to know what happened with the Council this weekend." Rupert nodded, and Darien recounted the meeting with Clara and the other masters.

About halfway through the tale, Vicky knocked on the door, announcing her return with refreshments. She passed out the coffee and set two blueberry muffins and a few clementines on the desk. Darien paused in his story long enough to thank her before she bowed herself out without a word.

"She's so thoughtful," Rupert said as he picked up one of the muffins.

"It's so nice to not have to stop a conversation because the help comes in." Darien picked up a clementine and split the peel open.

"So, you were saying the Council thinks that the Gray Courts could be involved in the murders?" Rupert muttered around a mouthful of muffin.

"Yes." Darien popped a piece of the fruit in his mouth.

Rupert stopped his chewing to stare at him.

"Rachael suggested that they might know something about it. There's a very limited list of people who could be the culprit. When you take out vampires and werewolves, you're left with fay or something really obscure—" Darien stopped his explanation and looked at the wolf staring at him. "What?"

"Nothing," Rupert looked away from the vampire. He knew Darien was special, but, other than coffee, he had never seen the man eat before. Rupert cleared his throat and collected his thoughts to continue their conversation. "Are you going to go to the Gray Courts and talk with the Queen?"

"Do you know anyone else who could?" Darien asked, hoping for some alternative.

Rupert shook his head "No, none of my wolves have been welcome there for a long time."

Darien could hear the regret in his voice. "Fay have long memories, but they're not totally heartless," he reassured the alpha. "I'm sure they'll forgive both the wolves and the vampires for their petty differences. Eventually." Darien sighed. He was afraid that getting the three groups together to work out their differences was going to take an act of several gods. Or one vampire with a really big stick.

"Well," Rupert drew the conversation back to the topic, "let me know how it goes."

Darien agreed, and the two men stood up. Escorting his guest to the door, Darien opened it to let Rupert out. "I'll call you when I know something."

Vicky looked up from her computer as the two men stepped out of the office.

"Have a good evening, Miss Westernly," Rupert nodded to her.

"And to you," she answered as the man left.

"The muffins were a nice touch," Darien said, complimenting Vicky's thoughtfulness.

"They were actually Sue's idea," she admitted. "But, I'll let her know they went over well."

Darien smiled and turned back to his office. Now that he had talked with Rupert, he needed to make arrangements to meet with the Queen of the Gray Courts. Visiting the fay was more taxing than any encounter with the vampires or werewolves. The fay were so formal about everything. He couldn't just intimidate the Gray Courts when they pissed him off.

Taking a deep breath, Darien pulled out a piece of parchment, so he could write a letter, requesting an audience with the Queen.

"You should have seen her out there, bumping and grinding between the hottest pair of twins I have ever seen!" Beth laughed as she filled Maggie in on the events of Monday night. The music of the club thumped around them as the four college friends sat in their booth at Alchemy.

"That was the best night I have had in a long time." Vanessa had the decency to blush at the memory.

Vicky held up her hand. "Stop right there. I don't want to know about your threesome with the pirate boys."

"But it was such a wonderful night," Vanessa teased.

"Did they stay all night?" Vicky asked, curious to see if they were vampires or minions.

Vanessa let out a forlorn sigh. "They left right after we were done," she confessed. "They said something about needing to get food before they went to work. I offered to cook, but they just laughed at each other and declined."

Vicky tried to keep the smile off her face.

Vanessa saw the smirk and glared a Vicky. "What about your two hotties?"

"What?" Vicky nearly choked on her drink.

"Yeah," Beth piped in, "you had two of the hottest guys in the club with you when you left."

Vicky blushed under the eyes of her friends.

"The one with dark hair was her *boss*," Vanessa smirked.

Beth gasped. "No way! I didn't recognize him." She shifted her attention back to Vicky. "What was he doing here?"

The red on Vicky's skin deepened. "I don't know," she lied. How was she supposed to tell her friends that he'd come out to tell the vampires she was safe to dance with?

"I bet he came out to see you," Maggie teased.

"How did he know she was here?" Beth asked.

"Maybe he's got a tracking device in that bag," Maggie answered, and the girls looked at the leather bag stuck in the corner.

"Don't be ridiculous," Vicky huffed. "Of course he doesn't. Why else would he need to call whenever he wanted something from it?"

"Maybe he just doesn't want you to know he's tracking your movements," Vanessa offered.

"Enough about my boss." Vicky closed the subject. "How was your night, Beth?"

Beth looked puzzled. "It was pretty good until you left."

"What happened?" Vicky asked.

"Well, the people around me started asking strange questions about you and your relationship with 'Master Darien'." Beth flashed air quotes around Darien's name.

"You know, I got the same thing," Vanessa added. "There were a lot of people calling him 'Master Darien'. I wonder if he's into S&M…"

Vicky rolled her eyes at the giggling girls. "What did they ask?" Vicky was interested in what the vampires wanted to know.

"Normal things, really: how old you were, how you knew Darien, how long you two had been together…" Vanessa answered.

"I got those too, but I also got some weird questions," Beth added. "What your favorite color was, your favorite food, and one girl asked what your dress size was. I stopped answering questions when someone asked where you lived."

Vicky's eyes widened in surprise.

Beth patted Vicky's hand reassuringly. "I wouldn't give my girl away like that."

"Thank you, Beth." Vicky was sure they would find out given half a chance. She made a mental note to watch her surroundings more carefully.

"What about the other hottie?" Maggie asked. "Who was he?"

"Yeah," Beth sat up straighter. "Who was the guy with the long, blond hair?"

Vicky blushed as she remembered her encounter with Elliot. "His name is Elliot, and he's a friend of Mr. Ritter's. He saved me from some creep on the dance floor," she offered.

"Why do you get all the luck?" Vanessa whined.

"Shut up." Beth smacked Vanessa's arm. "You had twins."

All the girls giggled into their drinks.

"Good evening, ladies." The group looked up to the face of a very handsome man with long, blond hair.

"Elliot!" Vicky squeaked as she recognized the vampire whom they had just been talking about. "What are you doing here?"

"I came to check out the nightlife." Elliot grinned at the girls.

Vicky quickly noticed that he was less fangy tonight.

"It's a pleasure to see you again, My Lady," he bowed gracefully to Vicky, causing her friends to ooh and giggle. "I have a group of friends with me this evening, if you ladies would like to come join us."

Vicky thought about declining the offer. She was still leery about dealing with vampires.

"We would love to!" Vanessa piped in before Vicky could say anything.

Elliot smiled. "They're over here." He held out his hand, pointing the way towards his waiting friends.

Vicky sighed and picked up her bag and drink before following the eager girls. Elliot offered her his arm and she took it so as not to be rude.

"I promise they're safe." He spoke just loud enough for Vicky to hear him.

She gave him a shocked look. "Did Mr. Ritter send you?" She couldn't keep all the suspicion out of her voice.

Elliot laughed. "No, My Lady, we truly happen to be here by chance." He smiled at her. "But I couldn't pass up the opportunity to get to know you better."

Vicky sighed deeply as they walked. "From what Vanessa and Beth tell me, a lot of people want to know me better."

"That's to be expected," he replied, shrugging. "Master Darien hasn't kept a human companion in a very long time."

"But I'm *not* his companion, I'm his secretary," she protested.

Elliot chuckled at her. "That may have been how it started, but he has 'taken you in', so to speak, so you're viewed by many as his companion" he explained. "There are lots of perks to being a master vampire's companion. Especially one as powerful as Master Darien."

"Perks?" she questioned.

Elliot laughed. "As long as it's okay with your master, you'll never want for company."

She blushed at the suggestion in his words.

"And, if you need it, a plethora of people will come to your aid."

"So... help moving furniture?" she said, raising a teasing eyebrow.

Elliot laughed again.

She was starting to like that musical sound.

"If that's what you need, then yes," he confirmed, and Vicky giggled.

Their conversation ended when they arrived at the tables containing Elliot's friends. Introductions were made, and the girls were soon out on the dance floor with eager partners. Vicky found a chair and deposited her bag into it.

"Will this be safe here?" she looked around at how open the area was. At least in the booth, the bag was stuck in the back, where someone couldn't see it easily.

"It'll be fine there," Elliot assured her. "No one will bother that bag."

She gave him a puzzled look and tucked the strap up, so it wouldn't catch on anything.

"Would you like to dance?"

He held out his hand, and Vicky allowed herself to be led to the dance floor, where her friends were already having a good time.

Vicky and her friends spent the rest of the night swapping partners with Elliot and his companions. As the night progressed, Vicky discovered that the group was made up of Elliot's personal menagerie and a few of Rachael's people. Elliot was the only vampire among them. When she asked why there weren't more, he grinned and informed her it was due to the werewolves in the club. Vicky spent the rest of the night looking for anyone that might be a werewolf, with no success.

⋘⦿⋙

"It's starting to get late, and I need to be heading home," Vicky informed Vanessa.

Her friend sighed. "Always the responsible one," Vanessa teased as she finished her drink.

"Some of us work for a living," Vicky teased back.

"But tomorrow is Sunday," Vanessa complained lightheartedly. "Is your boss making you work on Sunday?"

Vicky giggled. "Today is Sunday," she corrected, looking up at the clock showing one thirty. "And no, he's not making me work. I'm just used to going to bed much earlier than this."

"Good, I was going to have to have words with your slave-driver if he was making you work." Vanessa nodded. "He's already asking too much by making you carry that bag everywhere."

Vicky giggled at Vanessa's indignation. "I'll see you later." She hugged her best friend goodbye, and Beth and Maggie lined up for hugs, too.

When Vicky gathered up her bag to go pay out her tab, Elliot appeared at her elbow and offered her an arm. She took it without thinking, and he turned her towards the door. Making a slightly distressed noise, she looked back at the bar and her unsettled bill.

Elliot chuckled again, "It's already been taken care of."

Vicky's mouth worked in surprise.

"Another perk." Elliot explained.

"Did you?" she asked, and her escort shook his head smiling.

"Not by me," he held the door open for Vicky to pass through. "Master Darien's name holds a lot of weight in this town."

202

She looked at him, surprised.

"How are you getting home?" Elliot changed the subject.

"Well, I was going to catch the bus," Vicky pointed to the stop at the corner.

"Then, let me walk with you." Elliot led her down the street to the bus stop. "Do you always take public transportation?"

"I find it's easier than trying to keep a car in the city." Vicky shrugged as she headed to the bench. "The buses are fairly reliable, and if I've had too much, I can always get a cab."

Elliot nodded his approval.

"Should you really leave your group at Alchemy?" Vicky changed the subject.

"They can fend for themselves." He smiled. "I'm worried about your safety right now."

"I may not look it, but I can take care of myself," Vicky sassed at the vampire.

"I'm sure you can." He smiled and turned his attention to the night as the amusement slipped from his face. "There is something strange on the air tonight." He looked back at her and gave her a reassuring smile. "Besides, it would be improper to let a lady go home unescorted."

Vicky gave him a shy smile before looking back at the club in concern. "Will the girls be okay?" she worried out loud.

Elliot followed her eyes back to the club. "They'll be fine," he promised. "I've made sure they'll not go out alone, but it's not them I'm concerned about."

Vicky thought about this for a while as Elliot turned his attention back to the night. They sat in an odd silence until the bus pulled up a few minutes later.

"Here we go," Vicky said as she climbed onto the bus.

"That didn't take long at all," Elliot mused as he mounted the steps.

"Of course not," she informed him. "I have all the schedules memorized, and I know when to leave, so that I don't have to wait long at the stops." Vicky smiled at him.

"Smart girl." Elliot took the seat next to her. He looked around at the brightly lit bus. "It's been a long time since I've been on public transportation."

"Really?"

"The buses don't run after dark where I usually stay." Elliot shrugged.

They spent the rest of their trip talking about the differences in their cities.

Vicky pushed the button, and the bus pulled up to the stop just down the street from her apartment. "This is my stop," she told Elliot. "You may want to stay on the bus and take it back to the club. The next one doesn't come by for another hour."

Elliot waved the suggestion away. "I would feel better seeing you safely home," he informed her.

Vicky shrugged and led her escort off the bus and down the street.

"You really don't have to worry," she reassured him. "I live in a quiet area. You can get some trouble a few blocks over, but not here." Vicky kept her eyes open for anything out of the ordinary as they walked. She even looked down the alleyways between the buildings, in case something was hiding there.

"You can never be too careful at night," Elliot replied

as he looked around.

Vicky could feel the tension rolling off him. "This is me," she pointed to the brick building she called home. "Did you want to come in?"

Elliot shook his head, and Vicky could feel the tension drain away from him. "Just seeing you safely home is good enough." He bowed to her. "Have a good night, My Lady."

"Thank you." She smiled. "You have a good night, too."

Elliot watched Vicky walk up the steps and disappear into the doorway. He waited for a few moments on the sidewalk until the light in the first floor apartment came on before turning and starting back down the street. He was glad that she had made it home safely, but that nagging feeling wouldn't go away. It had been a long time since one of his premonitions had been wrong.

Elliot had only gone about half a block when an ear-shattering boom shook the night, and flames erupted from the building Vicky had just entered. He turned and ran back, cursing himself for not following the woman clear inside.

17

S MILING, V ICKY SHOOK HER HEAD AS SHE OPENED HER APARTMENT door. She was glad Elliot had walked her home. It had been a welcome change from having to make the trip on her own, and his company was very pleasant. She just wasn't sure what he was expecting to happen.

Flipping the light on, she stepped on something that hadn't been on the floor before she'd left for the club. Bending down, she picked up an envelope and looked at it. Her full name was scrawled across the outside, so she flipped it over and broke the seal. The card inside had the most beautiful picture of fall trees on it. Their fiery red and orange leaves glowed brightly in the afternoon sun. Vicky kicked off her shoes and took the card over to the lamp, so she could read what was written inside:

"For the good times we shared."

She read the words three times, trying to determine what they meant. There was no signature. Since there was nothing else in the card, Vicky shook the envelope and found something shifting inside. Puffing out the sides, she looked in to see a round disk. It wasn't thick enough to be a penny, but it was about the same size.

She dumped the brass coin out into her hand and hissed in pain when it hit her skin. She quickly dropped the hot object to the floor and turned her hand up to look at the burn. The disk hit the floor with a great explosion that threw Vicky back into the wall between the kitchen and bedroom doors. Spots filled her vision as she tried to hang on to consciousness. A sultry laugh filled the air as she was pulled away into senselessness.

⬥⬥◉⬥⬥

Heavy smoke choked Vicky as she shook the darkness from her mind. Coughing, she opened her eyes to find her entire living room engulfed in a raging inferno. She could hear banging and yelling from her front door, but there was no way she was going to get through the fire to open it. Vicky looked around the room for another way out, but flames blocked her path to the living room windows. Turning to get away from the heat, she found that her bedroom wasn't burning as hotly. Scooting towards the doorway, she tried to clear the pain from her head. She needed to think of a way out.

Vicky hissed as the flames licked at her leg and caught on the silk of her stockings. Batting at the fire, she crawled into the cooler area of the bedroom. The flames leapt after her as if they were alive, and she moved faster to get away from them. She smelled when the fire caught in her hair and beat at it, frantically, to get it out. When the flames were reduced to embers, Vicky stood up and rushed through the smoky air to the window that offered her escape. Releasing the lock, she pulled hard on the sash, but it wouldn't budge.

Fire bloomed on the curtains around her, and Vicky banged on the glass with all her might, trying to get the thin panes to break. She screamed in pain and frustration as blisters formed on the bare skin on her arm. Bending over slightly, she grabbed her chest as she coughed the smoke from her lungs.

Her hand landed on the strap of the messenger bag, still draped over her shoulder. Grabbing up the stout bag, she slammed it into the glass, repeatedly. On the fourth hit, the glass shattered with a loud pop and a strange hiss. The fire around Vicky subsided slightly, and she crawled out of the hole, cutting herself on the jagged shards of glass. The bag strap snagged on the broken framework and snapped as she tumbled to the fire escape in tears of pain and relief. Grabbing up the bag, she fell the five feet from the metal scaffolding onto the cool concrete of the alleyway.

The cry of her name and the pounding of feet met her ears. Vicky opened her eyes to see Elliot's blanched face looking down at her. Coughing harshly, she passed out under the vampire's gentle hands and the song of sirens in the distance.

Elliot dropped to his knees over Vicky's crumpled form. She was a mess. Blood and soot stained the parts of her that weren't burned. Pressing his hand to her chest, he prayed for a heartbeat. It was there, but not very strong. He rolled her up in his arms, considering his options. He could ensure that she survived by turning her, but he would have to do so and get out of there before the emergency crews got any closer. Then the question came to mind. Would Darien forgive him for turning her?

Closing his eyes, Elliot released his hold on his gifts. He really didn't like reading someone's life, but he had a feeling that this woman would be worth it. As his power washed over her, he searched for an answer. His mind brushed up against something that made him shiver, and he opened his eyes to look at her slackened face. Her future was riddled with branches that made the path unclear—choices that could change her life forever. There was only one thing he was sure about.

She would play a pivotal role in the life of one very old vampire.

Acknowledgements

First off, I have to thank my sister. When Amanda deployed aboard the USS George H.W. Bush (CVN 77), she was cut off from the fanfictions she loved. She begged us to send her reading material. Since I wasn't interested in some of the mash ups she requested I decided to write her a whole new story. And she wanted vampires.

I would like to that all of the many people that went into making this book. My mother, for the many hours on the phone bouncing around ideas and nursing plot bunnies. Laura, for beta reading, proofreading the original 180k word manuscript, and general encouragement. My father, for actually making it through the book and enjoying it. Krys, for putting up with the hours I spent playing on my computer as I worked through that first rough draft.

I have really appreciated the encouragement of those around me. Jackie and the employees at HobbyTownUSA, the guys at FRC, my family, my friends, and anyone else that had to listen to me ramble on for hours about the fictional characters gallivanting through my head.

I'd like to thank Melanie and the girls at Clean Teen/

Crimson Tree Publishing; Rebecca, Courtney, Dyan, and Marya. Thank you for taking a chance on an author with no experience and a manuscript that was way too long.

And finally, I'd like to thank the soldiers and sailors of the United States armed forces. You go out and give up so much so people like me can muck about safe at home. Thank you for your service. I pray you make it home safely.

About the Author

Originally from Ohio, Julie always dreamed of a job in science. Either shooting for the stars or delving into the mysteries of volcanoes. But, life never leads where you expect. In 2007, she moved to Mississippi to be with her significant other.

Now a mother of a hyperactive red headed boy, what time she's not chasing down dirty socks and unsticking toys from the ceiling is spent crafting worlds readers can get lost it. Julie is a self-proclaimed bibliophile and lover of big words. She likes hiking, frogs, interesting earrings, and a plethora of other fun things.